FIRESIDE

MODERN LEGENDS AND LORE

MOMS WHO WRITE

ISBN: 979-8-9851333-9-4

Cover art by Moms Who Write Team.

Edited by Brigid Levi, Allison Wells, and Moms Who Write.

Layout by Allie Gravitt.

Published by Moms Who Write LLC.

For permissions email contact@momswhowrite.org

momswhowrite.org

Table of Contents

Darkest Shadow

B. K. Clark

))》◐ᗕ(((

*M*ost people are afraid of the dark—but there are far worse things than darkness.

A bright beam of light clicks on and I jump, hiding my face inside the crook of my arm.

"There," someone whispers. "Do you see her?"

"Dear God," another voice says. "Look at her hands." Heavy footfalls thud and crunch against the floor.

"Turn off the light," I whimper, eyes burning. "I don't want to play right now."

"Hey, hey," a woman says, crouching down. "It's alright, sweetheart. I'm Officer Ruiz, and this is Officer Lawrence. We're here to help you."

My eyes snap up and snag on the corner of the room. "You can't help me." I hide under both my arms. "Please," I beg. "Don't make me play."

"You don't have to play anything," the woman says, still holding her stupid light. "It's all right."

"They'll make me." I hug my knees, palms rubbing against my shins. "If they see me."

"Who's they?"

I point a shaking finger at the corner. "Can't you see it?"

"See what?" She shines her light, and it lands on Lawrence.

I scream, "Turn it off!

Slowly both officers look in the corner and then at each other, eyes growing. I don't miss the way Lawrence holds his finger to the side of his head, twirling it.

Crazy. He's telling her I'm crazy. But he's never looked into the blacks of their eyes.

Heard their whispers.

"I'm going to check out the boy's room." Lawrence pulls out a cloth, covering his nose and mouth and heads down the hall.

"Sweetheart." Ruiz crouches down again. "I'm sorry if the flashlight frightens you. But the lights aren't working in here, and I need it to see. Do you understand?"

I swallow because that's the problem—she doesn't see. "What terrible sin have you done?"

"Excuse me?" She stares at me, and I recognize it. Only a flash, but the memory is there.

"Darkness always finds the darkness," I say.

"What's that supposed to mean?"

I point over her head. "It's found you."

"Ay!" She whips around with her light and lets out a nervous laugh when she sees nothing. "*Dios mío*, you scared me."

"Please." I try once more. "Don't move and turn off the light." She reaches out and pats my head. "I'm not afraid of my shadow."

"You should be."

She humors me with a smile. "What's your name?"

"Talia."

"That's a beautiful name." She smiles. "How old are you?"

"Twelve."

"Talia, can you tell me what happened to your brother?"

I don't answer her. My body shakes, and I rub my tender palms along my knees as I watch over her head. "It's closer."

She ignores my warning and moves again. "Can you tell me what happened to your hands?" She looks down at them. "Were you trying to pull him down? That must have been hard," she says. I swallow. "I read a report about your parents, too. Are you all alone now? Wasn't your aunt supposed to be staying with you?"

"They made her leave." The muscles below my mouth lose control, vibrating my bottom lip. "Now I hide from them."

"Who?" A loud clatter whips her around. The flashlight to the side of her gun shakes in her hands. "Who's there?"

"That one wants you to play. Don't play."

"Hush, child." She takes a crunching step over glass and her light lands in the corner. She freezes and I squeeze my eyes closed. He's whispering.

"Oh my God," she says.

"Paramedics will be here in five." Ruiz jumps and Lawrence lifts one brow. "You all right?"

"Fine." She rubs a trembling hand over her eyes. "Did you say five minutes? We've been here ten already."

"The joy of country living. You sure you're okay?"

"This place just gives me the creeps."

"Wait 'til you see the kid down the hall. I won't be sleeping for months."

Ruiz turns back to me and I startle. It's already begun. Her irises are bleeding black. "It always starts with the eyes," I say.

She rejoins me on the floor, rubbing her temples. "Enough with your spooky talk."

"But you saw the darkest one." I turn to her questioning face. "You looked looked into his eyes, and now it's too late. He's seen it."

"Seen what?" she snaps.

"Your terrible sin. My mama told me the eyes are the window to the soul," I say. "But he has none."

Three paramedics walk in wearing face masks and gloves, bags slung over their shoulders. They split, the two men going down the hall. To his room.

The female comes to me, and Ruiz eyes me before standing on shaky legs and spouting off information. "Multiple lacerations to her face, arms, legs, and knees. I think she's been crawling on this." She gestures to the floor covered in glass and splintered wood.

"What the hell happened in here?" the paramedic asks.

"Playtime," I answer.

She blinks at me a few times and darts a look to Ruiz. "And her hands?"

"I think she tore the skin off from the rope in the boy's room." She leans in, whispering something in the paramedic's ear who removes a needle from her bag.

But I don't care. My vision has blurred to see Ruiz, falling to the floor face first, tearing her hair. She claws at the wood, and her nails split backwards.

It hasn't happened yet, but it will.

They've whispered the plan to me.

A cry tears from my throat, and both women stop to look at me.

"Talia?" Ruiz says. "What is it?"

"I'm sorry." Tears soak my face. "I didn't mean to wake them. I just wanted to play."

A sharp prick hits my arm and I gasp.

"This will help you relax," the paramedic says, removing a needle from my arm.

"No, please." I look at Ruiz, and her eyes are solid black now. "No," I whimper and start to drift. That's when I hear it.

Ruiz screaming.

* * *

I blink awake and suck in a sharp breath. "No!" All my limbs are strapped down, and all I see is light. I convulse and yell, "RUIZ?"

Beeping turns erratic and there's a click of a door, and rushing feet. "Talia, you're all right. You're at the hospital. You were too violent in your sleep, and with your injuries, we didn't want you hurting yourself more."

My eyes dart all around me. My breaths come out in short bursts. "I can't see them. Where are they?"

"Where are who?"

"Umbra. Where are the shadows?"

She leans over me, and I shudder as the darkness follows her body over mine. "Is the light too bright?"

"Y-Yes."

"We'll be dimming them for the MRI. Hold tight." She leaves, taking her shadow, and I let out a shaky breath.

A nurse comes in and smiles at me. "Man, you're a wild sleeper," he says. "Made me want to see what's going on inside that head." He wiggles his fingers and says, "Now I will, muahaha."

I stare, wide-eyed and he belts a loud laugh. "I'm only kidding. Mostly." He winks.

I force a wobbly smile.

"Now listen, it's very important that you stay as still as possible. Can you do that for me?" He secures a strap over my head.

"Yes," I say because being still is what I'm good at. If you're still long enough, they forget you're there.

The table slowly glides me toward the tube with soft lights. A giggle catches my attention, and I look toward my feet.

Ring around the rosie, a pocket full of posies. A child's echoing voice sings and every muscle locks in my body.

"Relax, Talia." The doctor's distant voice finds me.

A series of loud beeps fades against the pounding of my heart and the blinking lights blur as he appears in my watery vision.

A boy my age stands at my feet. Long stringy hair covers his face down to his thin, pale shoulders. He grips one of my toes. "This little piggy went to market," his scratchy voice says as he moves it. "This little piggy stayed home." He laughs a hollow, throaty laugh and pinches hard. I wince.

"Come on, Tallie," he sing-songs. "Play with me."

I clamp down on the inside of my cheek until iron runs along my tastebuds.

Releasing my foot, he skips around the room, around a nurse who flips off the lights and doesn't see him. "Say, say my playmate," the boy sings. "Come out and play with me." He stops next to a light in the corner. "Taaallieee," he intones. "Look."

A small whimper slips between my pinched lips.

"Look at the bunny, Tallie."

I suck in a sharp breath, eyes glued to the white wall on the other side of the room. The boy no longer stands there, but it's there. A rabbit made from the shadow of a child's fingers, hopping across the wall.

My breaths come out in short bursts. My lungs ache.

The shadow grows.

Grows.

GROWS.

"Boo!" The boy pops back and I screech. He laughs, face still hidden behind his hair.

"Jimmy," I reach for him. "Please, stop."

He goes still, head tilting, hands lifting out at his sides. A bloody screwdriver clenched in his fist. "Didn't I say please?"

I gulp and gasp for air. "I did what you asked."

The hair over his face falls away and gaping sockets stare back at me. "Did you?"

My body convulses and a sharp pain seizes my chest. He holds a finger to his lips and smiles. "Shh. Let's play hangman."

. . . and I scream.

* * *

My eyes blink open again. I'm sitting on a chair in a bookshelf-lined room with a window and a heavy wooden desk at its center. A deep ache is in my chest.

"Talia?"

I startle at his voice.

"I'm Dr. Forrester. Do you know where you are?"

I shake my head. My sight snags on the afternoon sun sending beams of burnt orange light through the glass. It's been so long since

I've seen the sun, but it doesn't comfort me anymore.

It shows too much.

"You are at a state funded mental health facility," he says. "Do you remember coming here?"

I shake my head again.

"I have a theory about that." He smiles. "Do you want to hear it?"

He takes my silence as a yes. "You've suffered severe trauma, and I believe when it gets too much for you, you shut down." He taps his temple. "Up here."

"Talia?"

I startle and blink up at Dr. Forrester. "Yes?"

"It seems you blanked again when I asked if you remembered your heart attack during the MRI. So, let me ask you this instead. Do you remember Officer Ruiz?"

Slowly, I nod.

"Do you remember what happened to her after the paramedics showed up?"

"Screaming." My voice scratches, and I clear it. "I remember her screaming."

"Her partner said she saw something after talking to you and went mad. Something about a past sin coming back to get her, one she tried to make reparation for."

I inhale a deep, shaky breath. "She tore her nails on the floor," I say, and he nods. I repeat what I told her. "Darkness always finds the darkness."

He hums and picks up a pen, writing on a notebook in front of him. "Tell me about your hallucinations."

"I—" I swallow. "I don't have hallucinations."

He looks up, gray eyes steady on me. "You believe they are real then, these..." he reads over the paper in his hand, "shadow people."

I stare at the gleaming surface of his finished hardwood desk. A small brass clock sits at the corner, tick-tick-ticking away the time. The light shifts, and a shadow dances behind the clock.

"I don't believe," I say. "I know."

"And you believe they come from some sin you commit?"

"No," I bite my lip. "Not all. Some like to play. Only the darkest shadows are from sin."

"What if I were to tell you that sins had nothing to do with it. That after looking at your brain scan, I can tell you that these 'darkest' shadows you see are a result of a growing tumor."

I hold my breath and count *one, two, three...*calming my heart rate. The way I did when Jimmy cried at night. "Not from sin?" He nods, and my knee begins to vibrate. Is it possible?

Dr. Forrester leans forward, bony elbows propped on his desk. "Tell me about James."

The shadow behind his clock shifts over the shiny surface of his desk. My knee rattles against the floor in rapid fire as a rabbit hops across the surface. A bird takes flight.

I straighten and shake out my head. Tumor. A long hissing breath escapes me, and the shadows stop moving. "James is my brother," I say.

He nods. "Yes, and do you remember what happened to him before Officer Ruiz found you?"

My heel is a drumbeat. Beating against the hard surfaced floor.

"How about we try a different question. Do you see the shadow people now?"

"Yes and no." The clock on his desk keeps ticking. A black stag prances over the wall behind him.

"What do you mean?" he asks.

I glance up, and he's squinting at the clock I've been staring at. "I can also hear it breathing."

His palm rubs along his sharp, whiskered jaw, making mine itch.

I scratch them.

"Do you remember when you started seeing them, or rather, hearing them?"

I think about the first time. Jimmy and I jumping on my bed. The laughter. The nursery rhyme songs. He'd turned on my lamp and held his hands over it, making the shape of a rabbit, hopping. A bird flying across the room made me laugh. Then a deer with antlers. A dog barking and chasing a butterfly.

They were happy, the shadows. They loved making us laugh.

"Yes." I swipe at the tear rolling down my cheek.

I also remember how, too soon, Jimmy lost interest. Even though I begged him to keep playing with me, he said playing shadow puppets was for babies. He didn't want to do baby things anymore.

But I know the truth. My father's fists making him a "man." My mother doing nothing to stop it. Then the bedwetting started, and night after night, he kept me up, crying.

That's when the shadows changed.

A dog chases a butterfly over the top of Dr. Forrester's desk, and my eyes burn.

"It's okay, Talia."

"No," I whisper. "It's not okay."

"Can you look at me?"

"I-I'm sorry, but I have to watch the shadows, Doctor," I say as the butterfly takes off. "I have to be a good girl and play now."

"I thought we talked about the shadows. Your tumor."

I rub my palms down my thighs. Clanking chains yank them back and I stare down at the cuffs on my wrists. My feet are bound together.

"I see you finally noticed them," he says. "They're there for your protection."

"Protection from me?"

"That's not exactly what I meant. It's not because of some sin, Talia."

I rub my palms in short bursts.

"Talia, please stop that."

Warmth seeps over my hands, and I glance down and gasp. Trails of liquid red drip down my legs. "The blood." I rub it, and it only worsens the crimson liquid soaking into my clothes.. "There's so much blood!"

"Talia. There is no blood. You're reliving a traumatic memory."

I snap up to Dr. Forrester, and it's there, a shadow wrapping around his throat, leaving a rope burn.

"What is it?" he asks. "What do you see?"

What do you see...

What don't I see?

I quickly check under the desk, but it's not there. I check the bookshelves and the desktop and the corners. No shadow puppets. No shadows anywhere. "Oh no," I cry out, jumping up. My hands jerk down from the weight of my bonds. "Where is he?"

"He? He who?"

I rub and rub and rub. My hands are soaked now. "WHERE DID HE GO?" Sobs tear through me, and I see him do it. Dr Forrester's fingers curl underneath the desk to press the button.

All the shadows return at once, blowing me backwards. My legs hit the chair, and I fall into it.

"Talia, are you alright?"

"Can't you see them?" I scream.

"Yes, Talia." He stands and comes around the desk. "I see a young girl, traumatized by the death of her parents, whose aunt abandoned her and her twin brother, and who witnessed her brother's suicide. I see the scars on her hands from where she burned them on the rope trying to save him. I see you, Talia. And I'm here to help."

The door behind me opens, and strong hands take hold of my arms. "Wait," the doctor says, holding up a hand.

"It wasn't his fault," I tell him through the flood in my eyes. The black bird freezes on his wall. The dog stops barking on the desk, and I clench my teeth. "Do you know why the Umbra comes, Doctor?"

"Umbra? The Latin word for darkest shadow?"

"I don't know its meaning. Only that it comes with the worst sin."

"Again with the sin."

"Some sins are unforgivable."

"Does this have to do with your brother? Are you saying he killed himself over some sin?"

"I'm saying it's not his fault," I sniff hard. "He just didn't want to see the shadows anymore."

The black puppets emerge from the desk. The wall. The bookshelf, morphing together into it—into *him*. I lean back in the chair. "Jimmy, please," I whisper. "No more. I don't want to play anymore."

"You think your brother is here?" Dr. Forrester asks.

My head ticks to the side. "Where else would he be?"

"But he died, Talia. Remember?"

My laugh is watery and I choke on it. "I remember everything." Down to the detailed pattern of rippling soles on the bottom of his shoes as he dangled from the ceiling. The screwdriver still clenched in his fist. "That's why the Umbra came."

"But shadows aren't spirits. They exist only when an object obscures the light. See?" He holds up his ugly, stupid ticking clock to the sun. "Like this."

How does he not hear the truth in his own words? "And what happens when we don't let the light pass through us?" I slap my chest. "Tell me, Doctor, where do our shadows come from?"

"You're not evil, Talia. You're a victim. You're not blocking any light."

Slowly, my arm lifts till it's forced to stop, finger pointing. "Then why is my shadow behind you?"

He doesn't turn around, but lets out a long, tired sigh, nodding to the men holding me. A sharp prick sinks into my arm, and I wrench and writhe. The world blurs around the edges. "Why did you do that?"

My words leave my mouth, syrupy.

"I promised I'd help you, and I will," Dr. Forrester says. "The next time you wake, the tumor will be gone. I'm taking the hallucinations away, Talia. I'll prove to you that they were just shadows."

"How?" I don't get my answer, my vision slowly fading.

But not before the shadow behind him screams.

* * *

I wake with a gasp. I'm in a white room. Lights beam from the top and sides. All four corners open. No furniture or bed.

I push up to stand, holding out my arms, and move in a circle. "Where are you?" No matter how I move, I can't find them—find *him*.

There are no shadows.

No. Shadows.

Unbidden, it bubbles up—laughter. He did it. Dr Forrester did as he said and made the shadows disappear. My joy gusts out in a loud laugh. He was right. My sins don't block the light.

I look down at my scarred hands. I can still feel the burn of the rope. The blood caked to it.

"Were you trying to pull him down?" Officer Ruiz's words fill my mind. "That must have been hard."

"No." I answer her now. It was easy dragging him. It was easy when you're smart and use a pulley from Father's shed to lift his body. He kicked, one hand gripped the rope at his throat. The other still holding the bloody screwdriver.

I didn't hate him, my brother. I only wanted him to stop crying for the father who hit him. For the neglectful mother who died with him when they drove into a tree because they saw a shadow in the road.

My shadow.

Jimmy had wanted it to stop. The shadow puppets I'd awoken when he stopped playing with me had turned into monsters under his bed. He begged me to help him make it stop. So I told him it would help if he didn't see them.

And then I handed him a screwdriver.

I'm not crazy like Officer Lawrence said. I only did what had to be done. You see, the darkness had already been there in Jimmy's eyes, in his soul. Just like Officer Ruiz.

And when the shadows whispered to me how I could get all

that I wanted, I whispered back.

I slide down the blank wall, happy cries shaking my body. It's all over now. It was a tumor Dr. Forrester said, not a sin.

The fluorescent light above me flickers.

Flick.

Flick.

Off.

In the center of the room, it looms. A shadow.

A black shadow.

Darkness always finds the darkness. He whispers my words, stalking toward me.

I scamper backwards, tight against the wall. Jagged breaths wheeze in and out of me. "My sins don't block the light. My sins don't block the light."

"Tallie," he sing-songs, gaping holes staring into what I know are the blacks of mine. "I'm ready to play now."

Who's Next?
Tristan Tuttle

The dark shadow followed me.

This is nothing new.
Shadows follow everyone, obviously. That's how nature works.
So at first I thought it was my own, but I noticed that when I moved, it
. . . hesitated.
That's when I knew.
Right there in the lamplit attic hallway of my grandfather's house, I
knew I had made a mistake.

I only came here to clear out the house after my grandparents
disappeared.
She went first, and my grandfather followed shortly after, a pale
shadow falling over the house.

I thought it was just mildew; every old house has it.

The cops gave up trying to find my grandparents.
With no bank activity,
    no bodies discovered,
        nothing to tie them to anything other than disappearing into
        the ether.
The police released the house back to us once they went through it.
I know too much. I have seen everything relating to true crime Netflix
has to offer.
This was not normal.

But I shouldn't have opened the envelope; I shouldn't have read the

letter.
I know that now.

But when you find a letter in the bottom of an abandoned trunk,
     in the attic of the creepiest house you've ever been in,
          after a set of mysterious disappearances,
               what else are you supposed to do?

Ignore it? Probably.

Did I? Nope.

In my grandmother's scrawling handwriting, I read aloud her words,
"What's yours is mine."

But the energy of that letter was off. I know that because I am very
good at picking up vibes.
(My roommate asks me to vet every guy she brings home.)

The light in the room tilted and the shadow attached itself to me.
It didn't hurt. Just itched a little, but he is for sure connected at the
root.
Cinders fell out of the back of my shoes when I stood up.
I wrote it off as dust from the old attic and headed back down stairs.

I am every white girl in every scary movie, and now me and not-my-
shadow are irrevocably linked.

So that's cool, I guess.

He's very good though.
He never complains, he only occasionally growls, but he doesn't eat
much.

It's almost like I am walking in the sun all the time with a long shadow
behind me no matter which direction I face.

I've noticed that every so often he gets a little closer.
The long shadow is slowly getting shorter, his smoky fingers lacing
into my blonde hair and leaving ash behind.
That part's annoying.

He likes my feet.
The black ash has spread from my feet to my ankles now, and it's not going away.
I've washed, salt-scrubbed, and used every available product Bath & Body Works has to offer, yet it's not budging.
But I just wear high top sneakers, so no one can see. It seems fine.

Well, except for the fact that it's spreading up my legs.
But since it's winter, I can get away with wearing pants and if anyone sees the black ash tendrils climbing up my leg, maybe they'll think I'm not shaving for the winter.

Okay, look, it's made its way to my belly and there's no way to hide this come summertime. I look like an ashen wolfman. I know we live in a time of body acceptance, but this is greatly going to impede on my hot girl summer.

I'm having a harder time breathing now.
I think the ash is in my lungs.
My chest is tight and I'm getting scared.
I used my old inhaler, and it's only giving me temporary relief.

I can't hide it anymore.
My face is turning a pale gray.
My once dewy cheeks look desiccated, drawn.
I look like my grandmother.
Her skin also had this tinge before she disappeared.

What was it the letter said?

What's yours is mine.

I guess the shadow meant that literally.

Even my thoughts have become confused.
I find my mind going dark.
Instead of thoughts, I see swirls of ash and mist.
My being is swallowed up into the dying embers of the shadow.
I hear growls that seem to resonate from my own throat.
I can hear others growling too.

I don't think I'm his first.
There are other people in this mist of mind; my grandfather is here.
He is a demented version of himself. My grandmother stands next to him.
Their heads are cocked at an awkward angle and their teeth are set in an odd evil grin.
I feel myself sliding into the hazy void taking my place next to them.

All that is me is him.
We are all lost in his shadow self.

My brother comes to town tomorrow.
I can't wait to see him.

The Ten Little Lives of Adelia Mae

Britta Brown

harles twisted the handkerchief in his hands, already discounting the cloth as a waste. Stains like these would be near impossible to remove, and even if he thought it worthy of the endeavor, who was left to perform the labor?

"Josephine, the sweet thing, was easiest of course." Adelia Mae Dalton's bell-like voice bid him to attend her sermon. He did so, careful not to disrupt the fine bone china setting with the jouncing of his knee. Delicate lace folded over his thighs, the cloth too long for the round children's table where he sat, and across from him, Adelia Mae Dalton raised her cup. "Don't you agree, Father Crampton?"

"Do I—," he coughed, covering his mouth with his stained handkerchief. Phlegm stuck in his throat, and he fought to swallow it down. "Do I agree?"

Adelia Mae set her teacup down, layering her hands in her lap to look him in the eye. The pale pink button of her lips was pinched tight, her blue gentian eyes fixed to his paling face.

"Yes, Father. Do you agree about Josephine?"

He pinched his tongue between his teeth, searching for any hint, any tell, and then he took a chance. "Yes, dear Adelia, Josephine was a sweet little gir—,"

"No, Father Crampton. Do you agree that she was the easiest?"

Adelia Mae set her teacup down, clinking it against the saucer just this side of too hard. The sharp sound made him wince and to Charles's shame, a sticky sweat bloomed across the back of his neck.

"The easiest?"

"To kill," Adelia Mae emphasized. "A turn of the handle and a layer of pitch to seal the windows. It is a quiet way to go, or so my research led me to believe. One simply breathes in the gas and drifts away." She plucked at the embroidery on her collar. "The hardest part was blowing out the pilot light, what with my stature being as it is."

"Miss Dalton, are you implying that Josephine's death was by your hand?"

"Josephine, Mama, Thomas. . ." Adelia Mae blinked her glass doll eyes at Charles. "I only did what was necessary."

Charles tucked his handkerchief away and scrubbed his palms against his thighs, sweat darkening the woolen trousers. He swallowed—and swallowed again—as he looked at the porcelain features of the little girl christened by his own hand. The pert nose and wide eyes, alabaster skin and a dusting of freckles that hid the horror possessing her tiny frame. "Necessary?"

"The maids were the most difficult." Adelia ignored his question, pressing slender fingers to her lips. Her eyes glittered with what could have easily been misconstrued as soft humor, though Charles was beginning to suspect that Adelia Mae was incapable of such gentle emotion. "Always tittering and gossiping when they ought to have been working diligently. Did you know, Reverend, that it requires one thousand pounds of force to break a neck by hanging? Dr. Fitswhittle was hesitant to answer my query, but it was outlined quite clearly in his medical journal."

Charles followed the tilt of Adelia Mae's head towards her bookshelf. Three shelves of English pine carved with elaborate whorls and floral embellishments and laden with children's tales and parables. A bible, a book of Psalms, bound scandal sheets (no doubt stolen from the maids), and a large, leather-bound journal of medical inclination. The sort of book no little girl ought to possess, but there it was, direct from Dr. Fitswhittle's office.

Charles remembered the little mystery. All the books, ointments, tinctures, and instruments that had disappeared. He remembered the accusations and the red-eyed bootblack who was fingered for the crime.

And he remembered little Adelia Mae clinging to her mother's skirts, her cheeks flushed from the scandal.

"I felt rather silly when I realized that a full breaking of the neck was hardly necessary." Adelia Mae raised her cup, blowing across the surface of her tea and sipping delicately before she continued. "Strangulation is just as effective, and what better way to achieve my aims than to have the girls handle the matter themselves?"

Enola and Prudence had been found in the late afternoon, strangled by the bedsheets they were stringing on a line. Linen coiled into rope had been tossed over a low-hanging limb and wound around their throats, wrists bound at the back by their own apron strings. Enola had died screaming, or so Charles had interpreted when he was summoned to perform last rites over the bodies. Her jaw was slack, lips a bruised purple on a skin mottled with burst vessels to the degree it resembled one of Mrs. Creegan's blueberry scones.

Prudence had held out longer, or so the constable surmised. Her body lay in the dirt, legs crumpled beneath a lifeless form as if the girl's bones had given out.

"Ken the lass worked to keep her feet," Constable McLean had confided. "See how the other'n dances on her toes? When she gave herself over, the weight o' the body is what did in poor Pru." He scratched a bushy sideburn, watery eyes narrowed as he moved his attention from one body to the next. "Hanged by the dead weight of Enola, she was."

Charles had looked up from the deep scratches marring Enola's wrists, his stomach churning with the knowledge that her skin would be found beneath Prudence's nails. "Then how did Prudence end up in the dirt?"

"The jolly girl were nae a wee thing, was she?" Constable McLean toed her side with his boot, nudging the sturdy maid where she lay. "Less of Mrs. Creegan's baking and more perambulations around the property and we might nae be here, aye?"

"Father?" Adelia Mae's musical voice cleared the fog of memory from Charles's head. He blinked, bringing his hazy vision back into focus. A headache had begun to claw as the pieces of a wretched puzzle began to assemble themselves into a clear picture.

"Forgive me, Adelia Mae, but I find myself disinclined to believe your story."

She halted with her fingers reaching for the handle of the teapot. Slowly, oh so slowly, her eyes rose to meet Charles's own. "Oh?"

"It is impossible." He coughed again, grimacing at the rise of copper in his throat. "Enola and Prudence were two grown women, taller and stronger than yourself. My dear Miss Dalton, I bid you to recuse yourself of this confession, for none would believe it."

Adelia Mae sat back in her chair, poised like a doll placed for viewing. One hand rose to twine a finger around a pale yellow curl. "You haven't been listening, Reverend. Enola and Prudence were silly nags, always whispering over the scandal sheets and shirking their duties for the sake of a game."

"A game, child?"

"A game, Father." Adelia Mae released the curl, and it bounced beside her cheek as she smiled sweetly at him. "No harder to convince the ninnies to play a made-up game than it was to persuade Mrs. Creegan to allow my aid in the kitchen."

"Now Adelia Mae," Charles attempted to add sternness to his voice, the no-nonsense timbre he summoned with ease every Sunday, but he could not quite erase the warble of cloying fright that weakened his words. "Mrs. Creegan suffered a terrible accident, her death in no way pointed towards murder."

"Did it not?" Adelia Mae straightened her teacup and took up the pot.

The threatening headache crawled outwards, digging its claws into Charles's temples. He closed his eyes, massaging the ache as he recalled what he could of the scene.

There had not been much to perform last rites over, and even less with which one could identify the body.

Charred remains and an overturned pot. The grease covered skirts and shoes with the obvious wear of having been worn too long on bunioned feet. Although, Dr. Fitswhittle had mentioned there was something about the skull. An indentation in the bone that spoke of trauma to the head.

"Blunt trauma, likely caused by a curved instrument such as a cast iron." The good doctor had confided in a low tone. "It was no secret that Mrs. Creegan was disliked by that soft maid of theirs. Perhaps she was refused one scone too many."

"Albert," Charles had admonished the doctor, but Fitswhittle only smiled in that patient way of his and raised his hands.

"A cruel jest. My apologies, Reverend." Snapping his medical bag closed, Dr. Fitswhittle had made haste towards the door, eager to leave the gruesome scene behind. "It is possible, even probable, that poor Mrs. Creegan was the victim of foul play, but who is left in the household to blame? Mrs. Dalton is incapable of leaving her bed after the passing of little Thomas, and the middle child is content with picking flowers and working on her embroidery. One could no more accuse the dulcet poppet of such violence, much less the strength required to be the cause of such trauma, than one could blame a squirrel." He looked pointedly at the brittle dent on Mrs. Creegan's blackened skull. "And for all my poor humor, I have it on good authority that Prudence prefers her entertainment to be of the pious sort. Is that not right, Father?"

Charles had left then, blustering his way from the room and the subtle accusation in Dr. Fitswhittle's tone. The Dalton home was a sprawling manse, and, in short order, he had gotten lost among the hallways. The ether-induced moans of Mrs. Dalton had forced him from one wing, and it was by the grace of God that his ear picked up the tiny grunts and muttered curses which had led him into the entry hall of Wyborn Manor. He had hovered there in the shadows at the edge of the hall, stricken by the image of little Adelia Mae hefting a broadsword into the gauntlets of a suit of armor.

"More tea, Father?" The girl tipped the spout against the edge of his cup, her brows tilted upwards just so as she awaited his answer. Charles parted his lips to reply, gaze falling on the tremor of her arm and the delicate, fine-boned wrist.

"Yes, please, Miss Dalton." The headache had grown worse and his throat held a curious itch. Another cup would help to clear his muddled thoughts. Another cup to erase all suspicions and dismiss the claims of the child. "Very kind of you."

"It is important in trying times such as these to keep one's head." Adelia Mae steadied the pot with both hands as she poured, one at the handle, the other supporting the base. Still, the bone china spout *tink-tink-tinked* against the rim of his cup, too heavy for the girl weakened by tragedy. "Papa was always best at remaining calm. Even as he bled out, he was ever so calm." The pot was raised higher by her hand, the last of the tea flowing from the spout and bringing with it flecks of leaves as they encountered the dregs. "Stoic, down to the last drop."

A weakness overcame him then, and Charles's hand shook from the sudden awareness that every word Adelia Mae was saying she believed to a degree that begged him to recognize the truth of her confessions. Tea sloshed up and over the rim of his cup, spattering against the tablecloth. He stared down at the growing stain, a brown kernel of rot festering from the heart of the fabric, crawling over the delicate lace and threatening to consume the purity of the whole.

"A shaving accident," he murmured.

"A slip of the wrist," Adelia Mae agreed. "A young lady can hardly be expected to hold a straight razor steady on her first attempt."

Charles clenched his jaw and made to rise, but his movements were clumsy. Shock, he told himself. Fright at the damning words of an innocent. She had seen too much, bearing witness to as much death as she had. It was only to be expected that in her grief, young Adelia Mae would take the responsibility upon herself as the last Dalton in a family of tragedies. The pressure she must feel to maintain the stiff upper lip and poise, to remain calm in the face of such macabre scenes. First the baby Thomas, and next the mother. The cook, the father, and the eldest sibling. The maids and housekeeper.

"You need not burden yourself with the weight of blame, Adelia Mae," Charles forced through a tightening jaw.

"But that would be un-Christian of me, Father." She dabbed at the growing stain on her tablecloth. A futile endeavor, but one she nevertheless undertook with the steel-spined purpose of a true Englishwoman.

A muscle panged in Charles's chest to see an adolescent forced to mature before her time. He loosened his collar and rubbed at the space with a knuckle as yet another pang drove deep into the tissue surrounding his heart, seeking to ease the cramp that set his pulse into an erratic flutter.

"And I am a diligent pupil when it comes to the practicing of my faith. Mama always said it was best to acknowledge our guilt and confess, and as you yourself reminded in last Sunday's service, 'If we confess our sins, He is faithful and just to forgive us our sins and to cleanse us from all unrighteousness.'"

"Yes, but Miss Dalton, were you truly responsible for their weighted crimes, for—for murder—," Charles shuddered, the muscles of his cheeks spasming at the dreadful thought, "you must recognize that the sins to which you confess are beyond forgiveness."

"'Though your sins are like scarlet,'" Adelia Mae cited the scripture, "'they shall be as white as snow; though they are red like crimson, they shall be as wool.'" She sipped from her cup before clasping it in both hands and engaging Charles with a beatific smile. "Isaiah 1:18, Father."

"Now, Miss Dalton." He rapped knuckles against the table, rattling the bone china as he raised his voice. "I shall hear no more of this self-condemnation. None would blame you for the tragedy that has befallen your household. You were right to call upon me, dear girl, for it is my duty as shepherd of a flock to see you through this time of mourning, but you are not to blame for the deaths of your family. Your mother miscalculated in her own grief, your brother Thomas succumbed to fever and watery bowels—"

"My brother Thomas died swaddled in a typhus-ridden blanket from the tenant farmers down the lane," Adelia Mae corrected, the smile still firmly affixed to her face. It did not belong there, that wide,

Cheshire grin driving unnatural dimples into apple cheeks. It was a merriment which illustrated the wrongness of the scene and the mutual discomfort of the participants in this play. "I gathered the scrap before all the goods of the household could be burned. Waiting out his death was most difficult, if I may speak so candidly. Drowning him would have been easier. Or perhaps a pillow over his face as he slept. He was always crying in his crib, and it would have been easy to ascribe the death to negligence on behalf of dear Prudence or poor Mrs. Appleton."

Charles blinked, and the image of the housekeeper crumpled at the bottom of the stairs swam before his eyes. Her neck bent at an unholy angle, the puddle of blood in which she lay, and little Adelia Mae clinging to the banister with a white-knuckle grip.

"She tripped."

Those whispered words had echoed in the hall, curling around the timber framing and rattling the stained glass before worming their way in Charles's ears and giving birth to a suspicion he dared not acknowledge in the moment. Those same words had pulled him up from where he crouched beside Mrs. Appleton, his fingers wrapped in a handkerchief as he felt for a pulse, cajoling Charles with the promise of comforting an unfortunate child.

"Mama only had herself to blame." Adelia Mae's voice, now absent the delicate ringing of youth, tore through the grim memory. Charles swept a hand across his brow, clearing away sweat that beaded along his hairline.

The conversation had disturbed him, overheating the Reverend in his seat, though the late winter day was cold and the window propped open. A crisp breeze billowed the curtains, sending filmy cream voile reaching into the room. Charles shuddered and bent away from the window lest those curtains find their way around his throat.

"How—," he rasped, his jaw tightened by tension as he restrained himself from bursting from the chair and fleeing the chamber. "How so?"

Adelia Mae fixed him with a pitying expression, as though the ten-year-old had expected him to be quicker, more intrepid, and resolute in taking her supposed confessions. He understood what the adolescent was building towards without her needing to state the matter clearly, as though she were conversing with an imbecile.

"Had she not relied so heavily on ether to soothe her heartache, I would not have had such easy means of terminating her grief as I did." The last Dalton straightened in her chair, shoulders rolling back and her spine arching forwards, the young miss attempting to make herself taller. More adult and firm in her wretched claims. "Though I shan't presume to expect any leniency in judgment for my having allowed Mama a swift and easy departure from this world. It is only that I could not bear to see her suffer, what with all that followed. It was best that she, like Josephine, drift away into sleep and then..."

She fluttered her fingers from where they lay against the table, those soft blue eyes growing distant and, unless Charles was succumbing to the spell this child cast over all around her, regretful.

Digging within the pocket on her pinafore, she retrieved a vial and settled it next to the now empty teapot. Charles read the label, recognizing the name as one of Dr. Fitswhittle's missing concoctions. His mouth ran dry, his bowels cramped, and his jaw locked firmly in place, capturing the shout which rose in his throat.

"Ten lives." Adelia Mae pursed her lips, her own voice choked from the effort of forcing the words. "Ten little lives that entered this world screaming and left it with a whimper and a sigh."

"But. . ." Charles reached for his teacup, seeking something tangible and solid in a world that had gone blurry at the edges. His fingers brushed the handle and sent the bone china clattering to the ground. It shattered against the wooden floor, fine shards shooting out in all directions. He winced at the mess. Mrs. Appleton would be livid. She was always berating Charles for being a doddering old fool, more at home in his rectory than with a woman. Incapable of the gentleness the softer sex required.

Mrs. Appleton at the bottom of the stairs with her head turned the wrong way around.

Clumsy fingers pincered above the saucer, closing around a teacup handle that was no longer there. Distantly, his mind recognized that the cup was shattered. No more. Gone like the rest of the Dalton family and their household, but that message had not quite traveled down to his hand. "But you have only accounted for eight lives, Miss Adelia Mae."

"Of course, Reverend Crampton." She set her own cup down and regarded him with that hollow blue-eyed stare. Her skin had taken on a damp, spongy appearance, like a vanilla tea cake left out on a humid day. Delicate hands folded in her lap, the fine silk of her gown wrinkling beneath a staunch grip as she gazed back at him with her pained rictus of a smile. "Why else do you think I invited you to tea?"

Bell House

A Bell Witch Retelling

Jennifer Dove Lewis

Betsy clasped her hands tightly over her sister's ears. Esther was sleeping, but Betsy knew her sister's shallow breaths and restless movements meant she was lost deep in a nightmare. Esther was always lost in a nightmare. But Betsy held her hands tightly over her sister's ears because the real nightmare was happening right here in their room. The scratching in the walls had been going on for hours, and Betsy knew they would soon stop. Before the dark night turned grey and light began to slowly filter into their room, the noises would stop and the real terror would begin.

* * *

"This has to stop, Mama," Betsy pleaded, grabbing her mother's arm and twisting her toward the table. "Look at her! Let's leave. We can pack everything up and go right now while he's out in the field."

"And where are we going to go, Betsy?" her mom yelled back. "Where will we go? Your daddy may not be the best father, but he's a good provider. He keeps food on the table and a roof over our heads," Lucy said. "He loves us."

"This ain't love," Betsy replied. "Look at her arms. Look at her!

She's wasting away to nothing and stays locked up inside herself. And I can't sleep with that thing in our room. I feel like I'm losing my mind, Mama. We have to get out of here." She finished, picking up her sister and walking out of the room.

"We have to eat, Betsy," her mom called pleadingly after her, her voice low and sad.

Betsy knew it wasn't her mama's fault. She was just as much a victim in this as anyone. She would never be able to stand up to her husband, Clarence. No one could. It still hurt, though. For once, Betsy wished someone in the family would just listen and care about what was happening to her and Esther.

"So that's all she is to you, a meal ticket? She deserves better than this," Betsy said to her mother's back, watching as her mama's shoulders slumped forward, knowing she had hurt her. Not caring. Betsy just couldn't care anymore.

She could hear her mom behind her as she walked out of the room, carrying on in the kitchen as if nothing happened. When Betsy came back in later, there would be a pot of beans on the stove and a cake of cornbread cooling on the counter. Mama would be canning tomatoes and green beans and pickled okra, and Betsy would tie on an apron and help her. Nothing would change if she left it up to Mama.

Betsy shifted Esther to her hip and grabbed some sage on her way up the stairs. She lit it and waved the clump of dried leaves in front of her as she climbed past the second level and into the attic where she shared a room with her sister. She tucked the little girl into her bed and began lighting candles. Although it was daytime, the attic had only one tiny window, and it stayed dark in their room all the time. Esther didn't seem to mind. In fact, Esther didn't seem to care about anything. She had been lost in her own world for over a year now, ever since Bennie died. Esther had loved that little baby, carried him around like he was her own little doll. Esther was only a tiny thing herself, but she saw herself as a mama to that boy. When he died, Esther stopped talking. Barely anyone noticed except Betsy.

* * *

The next morning, Betsy carefully dressed Esther and herself, and they walked downstairs together, hand in hand. Esther squeezed closer as they walked into the kitchen. Jonathan, their oldest brother, stood leaning against the counter, coffee in hand. He sneered at them as they sat down at the table.

"How's the little mute this morning?" he asked, looking toward their other two brothers who laughed at his joke.

Cade looked over at Betsy, then dipped his head. She knew he only went along with it because he was afraid of Jonathan. She didn't fault Cade for that. He glanced back up and she smiled at him. Cade was only ten and not yet ruined by her daddy and Jonathan. She hoped to keep some measure of kindness in him, but her daddy tried to beat it out of him every chance he got.

"She's not a mute," she replied, looking directly at Jonathan. She wasn't afraid of him. "She misses Bennie."

"Bennie's been gone over a year," her brother spat out. "She needs to get over that shit."

Betsy saw her mom flinch at Jonathan's words, but she continued wiping the dishes like she hadn't heard him. Her mama hadn't been the same, either, since they lost Bennie. He died of croup, and Betsy would never get the sound of his cough out of her mind. Or the silence when he stopped. Maybe that was when Mama stopped caring.

"Her real problem is you, Betsy. You carry on like there's demons in the closet. How's she supposed to sleep? Ain't no wonder she don't talk. She's scared of her own shadow," Jonathan continued, moving closer to Betsy.

Betsy backed up against the wall, feeling trapped. Jonathan pushed himself up against her and shoved his fingers up under her chin, forcing her to look up at him.

"Maybe you need to sleep in my room, Betsy. Give her some peace away from your horror stories for a while," he whispered, not quiet enough that mama didn't hear it, but low enough the other kids didn't pay attention. "Or, if you don't want to, maybe Esther does," he finished, leering at his little sister.

Betsy's stomach lurched. Jonathan was just as evil as the thing in the closet, worse in some ways. Betsy struggled to turn her face away from him, his rancid breath causing her to gag as much as his words.

The door slammed, and they all straightened up and shut up as Clarence Bell walked in. Jonathan stepped away from Betsy and leaned against the counter eating an apple as if nothing happened. Clarence looked around the room at each of them, his eyes daring anyone to move or speak as he wiped beads of sweat from his forehead. He had been out in the fields for hours already. Dirt caked the bottoms of his boots and left a muddy trail through the house. Betsy knew Mama would spend most of the afternoon wiping up that dirt because if

Daddy saw a speck of it come suppertime, there would be hell to pay.

"Well, come on then, we're gonna be late," he said finally, turning back toward the door. Everyone followed him. There were many things Clarence didn't tolerate, but being late for church was at the top of the list.

They all walked in together half an hour later and everyone's eyes turned toward them as they took their seats up front. They all talked, Betsy knew they did, but no one dared let Clarence know. The Bell family filed in quietly, each grabbed a hymn book, and opened to page thirty-one. Pastor Clemens always started with the river.

"Shall we gather at the river, the beautiful, the beautiful, the river. Gather with the saints at the river, that flows by the throne of God."

Betsy sang pure and clear. She wanted God to hear her voice, to see her. She needed His guidance as she made plans—plans no one knew but her. But today, she would speak them into the world, and there would be no turning back.

The pastor went on for two hours. He pounded his fists on the pulpit and spoke of hell and damnation. He talked about lies and the danger of opening yourself up to evil. He looked right at Betsy as he said this part, and she looked right back at him. She knew if Daddy saw it she'd pay for the impertinence, but she also knew what was true and what wasn't. She knew what she saw at night when the candles burnt out and the shadows descended. She knew the wrinkled old hand that reached up from under the covers and pinched and scratched Esther so hard she bled was not of this world. Their screams and pleading had gone ignored for years. Ridiculed. They were called witches by the kids in town, liars by their brothers, and stupid whores by their daddy. God only knew what the townspeople said. And Mama just kept quiet. She never spoke a word in their defense. Betsy had had enough.

The kids were allowed to walk home from church alone. It was one of the few times Betsy felt somewhat normal. Her friend, Hattie, fell into step beside her at the end of the church parking lot.

"Esther's arms are a mess," Hattie said, reaching for the little girl's arm and giving it a gentle kiss. "You gotta get out of there, Betsy."

They had this same conversation every Sunday. Hattie was the only one who believed her, the only one who wanted a better life for Betsy and her little sister. She was their only true friend and ally.

"We're leaving tonight," Betsy whispered, looking around first to make sure they were alone.

Hattie stared at her wide-eyed, not saying a word.

"Say something, Hattie," Betsy begged, her heart racing at having said the words.

"Maybe you shouldn't go," Hattie said, sounding as scared as Betsy felt. "How would you do it? And where would you go?"

"You're always telling me I should leave, Hattie," Betsy said, incredulously. "We have to leave. That thing is killing her, and nobody believes us."

"Betsy, I do believe you, I truly do. But..." Hattie began, but Betsy cut her off.

"But what, Hattie? You believe me but you don't?" Betsy spat out. "You know it's true. You know I ain't making this up. And just look at her," she said, pointing to little Esther.

The little girl walked silently, eyes fixed straight ahead, with no expression to indicate she heard or understood anything going on around her. Her eyes were empty of all emotion, and wide dark circles surrounded them. Hattie stroked a hand down the back of the girl's head, smoothing tangles in her hair. She smiled, but Esther didn't acknowledge it.

"How are you going to do it?" Hattie asked finally, reaching to take Betsy's hand in her own. "I can help."

"No," Betsy said right away. "I don't want you there. If my daddy thinks you're involved . . . "

She didn't finish the thought, but Hattie knew what she meant. Clarence was a hard, hard man. Nobody crossed him.

The girls continued walking in silence until they got to the river that ran between their houses. There they sat together on a rock protruding out across the water. Betsy loved this spot. It was the only place in the world she felt at peace. She watched a leaf float lazily by, mesmerized as it dipped and turned around the rocks and fallen branches. She thought about her plan. Esther couldn't make it much longer. They had to leave soon, and Betsy was fine with that. She couldn't get out of that house fast enough.

Hattie went her way, and Betsy and Esther finished the short walk home in silence. As they came around the bend, Betsy saw everyone was already there. The women gathered together under the willow sipping tea, whispering stories about the very house they rushed to visit every Sunday. The men stood smoking and talking, Clarence at the center of it all. All these people who shunned and ridiculed them in church, couldn't wait to get their fill of the Bell house every week. Clarence ate up the attention. He also ate up the money that made its way into the little metal bucket by the door as people wandered into their house. He always said loudly how he didn't want a penny, wouldn't dare ask anyone to pay for a nice, Sunday visit. But they all knew what was expected, and their morbid curiosity kept them coming back every week.

Betsy steeled herself and squeezed Esther's shoulder. This was one of the worst parts. She knew she had to perform, knew her silence and fear at the retelling was just as much a part of the show as the stories themselves and she despised every single person who took part in it. She glanced over and saw her daddy staring at her, a smile on his face for Pastor Reese, but hatred in his eyes for the girls who were showing up late to the show. All these people were here to see the girls. Their room was the one haunted. Their arms and legs were the ones pinched and bruised. They were the ones damned and possibly possessed. The talk of the town. The evil witches disguised as innocent girls. Betsy saw her mama standing by the porch, wringing a handkerchief in her hands, watching her husband with fearful eyes. She saw Betsy and waved her over, urging her to hurry up.

"There's my girls now," Clarence said jovially, reaching to put an arm around Betsy's shoulders as she got close. He pulled her into his side, and she had to fight the urge to pull away. She could smell the sweat and evil seeping through his shirt, the whiskey on his breath, and the sweet smell of tobacco. She smiled at the people crowding around, acting the part. This was the last time. She would tell them everything, then to hell with all of them. She and Esther may not make it out in the world on their own, but they were done trying to make it here.

"Betsy, what is it? What do you think's in there?" Miss Grayson asked. She was the organist at church, a sweet, grandmotherly type. She was practically salivating for the details.

"It's an old lady," Betsy said matter-of-factly. That's exactly what it was. She didn't need to make anything up.

"What does she look like?" another woman asked, her eyes wide with fear and excitement.

Betsy hesitated at that question. She didn't know exactly how to describe the woman. She wasn't always easy to see, it was more of a knowing. She and Esther just knew. But that would sound like a lie, or like they were making it up. So she told them what she did know.

"She's really dark, like a shadow. I think she wears a green dress, but it's hard to see in the dark. She's small—smaller than me—and her hands are wrinkled and cold. They're strong, though, her hands. Strong as any man's," Betsy finished quietly, wishing Esther didn't have to hear any of this. She could feel her sister trembling beside her. The women in the crowd smiled gleefully at the frightful story with no concern at all for the girl telling it or the one cowering behind her.

"Did she come last night?" a little boy of about ten asked. Betsy didn't usually get mad at the little kids. She knew they were curious and only doing what the grown-ups were doing. But she didn't like to answer their questions. She never lied, though. She told Daddy she'd give them a scary story, and the truth was scarier than anything she could make up.

"She came this morning," Betsy said. "She always comes just as the sun's coming up. It's dark in our room, though, so it's still hard to see her."

"What did she do?" the same boy asked, so quietly Betsy could hardly hear him. He was hiding behind his daddy's legs, holding on tight but still peeking around to hear the answer. Betsy was lost for a moment, watching them. The little boy's daddy held a strong hand on his head, protective, his fingers slightly over his son's ears as if to block out anything horrible he might hear. That was all Betsy ever wanted in her whole life, someone to protect her. She didn't want to scare the boy, but she was also jealous. She was suddenly angry at him, this boy who had everything, when she and Esther had nothing but misery.

"Me and Esther was curled up in the bed, as far in the corner as we could get," she began, wrapping her own hand around Esther's head and covering her ears just like the little boy's daddy did. "Our room's up there," she continued, pointing up to the tiny window in the attic. "It's dark in there all the time, so I had a candle lit. Esther was sleeping, so I pulled the blankets up around her, tucked them in tight all around her feet. You never want to leave your feet out."

Betsy paused, thinking how to tell the next part. It was hard to describe how it happened, and she knew none of them really believed her. But she wanted them to believe it. She wanted them to know the truth, so when she and Esther were gone they would all feel bad. They should all be ashamed. The church was supposed to wrap itself around the children, protect them. She wanted the truth to be out there so big and bold they had to question what they knew to be true when the girls were gone.

"She reaches up under the covers," Betsy continued. "I can't ever see her when she first comes. She slides out of the closet and up to the bed, only a slither of a sound. Like every time, I saw the covers move this morning, and I tucked them all back in tight, as tight as I could get them. I pulled Esther's legs up under mine. She's always worse on Esther," Betsy said, looking down to see if her sister was listening. Esther had her eyes closed and her head leaned against Betsy's leg. Their daddy was looking at them with a big smile on his face. He liked Betsy's story. She hated him more in that moment than she ever had.

"I can't ever keep her out, though. Once she starts reaching up, it's only a matter of time before I feel her hands. They're icy cold and dry. I could feel her hands and I started kicking at her, but she still got Esther's leg. She pinched her so hard blood came this time. Then, when Esther started screaming, that's when I saw her. She came up from under the blanket, and for just a second, I saw her face. She smiled at me, her teeth rotten inside her mouth. I pulled Esther close and we closed our eyes hard until she left. It was a long time. She stays and looks at us for a long time."

Betsy finished the story and the crowd was silent. She knew they wanted to think Betsy and Esther were witches or possessed or just making things up, but she also knew they kind of believed her. Betsy hoped they all had nightmares that night.

"They're everywhere. It's not just her, there's more of them. We can hear them scratching in the walls. There's one under the bed, but he never comes out. They're in your houses, too, you just don't know it."

At the last part, the little boy who had asked questions screamed, and his daddy pulled him real close again, picked him up even. Betsy hated every single one of them with every fiber of her being.

That night, Betsy helped her mama wash the dishes. They stood side by side silently working, never once looking at each other. Betsy was sorry for what this would do to her mama. She and Cade were the only ones Betsy cared about. The rest of them were just as evil as this house. When they finished up, Mama took Cade and left for Mrs. Capon's house. Mama was a midwife, and Mrs. Capon's labor had started. Betsy had passed on the word to Mama when she came in from feeding the goats. Mama always took Cade with her. She loved him the most—Betsy knew it—and that was fine. They would need each other after this night. She watched them walking down the path toward the river, sorry for her lie but glad they were gone. The Capon's lived about a mile up the river, and it was slow moving in the dark.

Betsy went back inside and gathered up Esther from the couch. Daddy was sleeping in his chair, and Betsy knew from his deep snores he was out for the night. The girls went quietly up the stairs, Betsy waving the sage back and forth as she went. She locked their door and tucked Esther in like she always did. Esther rolled over facing the wall and went right back to sleep. The early hours were the only ones she got, so Betsy always got her down as early as possible.

Betsy reached under the bed and got out the suitcase she found in the shed. It was old and dirty. She'd cleaned it the best she could, but it still had black marks in the creases and smelled of old dirt. She put as much of their stuff in it as she could. She added in some food she had been stealing the past few days. She had a few big hunks of bread, some cheese wrapped up tight in cloth, some dried meat from daddy's stash. She had stolen the meat when her daddy was packing it for his lunch, a little at a time. She had some apples, too, and had managed to find a couple small pieces of candy she hoped Esther might eat. Betsy thought once they left, Esther might get better. She had to get better. They would be all alone in the world, and Betsy couldn't bear it if Esther never talked.

She waited a long time, until the house was quiet, then slowly got up and walked around the room. She put her ear right up to the wall. She could hear the scratching and the whispering.

"Who's in there?" she asked, knocking lightly on the wall in several places. "Why are you doing this to us?"

No one answered, but she thought the whispers stopped for just a minute, like someone was listening. She looked back over at Esther to make sure she was still sleeping, then pulled out the large knife she had taken from the kitchen. She wrapped a towel around the end, brought it up over her head, and slammed it as hard as she could into the wall. The walls were thin, rotted through from years and years of leaky ceilings. The knife ripped out large chunks of plaster. For a moment, it was like time stopped. The air became still and quiet, and the hair stood up on Betsy's arms. She looked back and saw Esther sitting up in bed, staring at her. Betsy turned back to the wall and started stabbing again, over and over.

The house was screaming, that was the only way she could describe it. A thick, black fog filled the room, and Betsy could no longer breathe, her lungs refusing to pull in air. She grabbed Esther and the bag, unlocked the door as quickly as she could, and sprinted down the stairs. The sound was excruciatingly loud, but Betsy thought it was in her head, hers and Esther's. The boys' doors remained closed, and she didn't hear Daddy downstairs, but Esther was pushing her little hands as hard as she could against her own ears. Betsy kept running as quickly as she could with Esther until they were out the front door. She ran to the edge of the yard and put the girl down, along with the suitcase, then ran back to the house. She had planned the whole night; she knew what to do and where everything was. Within minutes, she finished what needed to be done and turned to run back to Esther.

The house was old and brittle, the wood barely hanging on in places. Once the fire started, it took over fast. The whole thing was up in flames within minutes. Betsy picked up her little sister and hugged her close.

"It's okay now, little dove. It's okay. We're getting out of here," she whispered.

The sounds coming from the house were louder now. The screams from the walls all mixed up with the screams from her brothers. Betsy waited until she heard the one thing she had been waiting for, her daddy's yells as he tried to make his way out the door. Everything was locked up tight, though, and Betsy knew they would never make it out. Betsy smiled at the sound of their screams.

She didn't know what evils the world held for them, but she knew the evil inside that house would be gone tonight.

She picked up the suitcase and turned away. For the first time in years, she felt free. She didn't know where they were going, but they would keep walking and walking, until they got to the next town. Betsy had enough money for a couple of train tickets and some food. They could make do with that for now.

They walked on in silence for what felt like hours. Betsy's feet were sore and tired, but she wasn't ready to stop. They would go on a little farther. The sun was just beginning to break over the horizon, and she could see an old barn way up ahead. They would stop there until nightfall.

Betsy felt Esther stir in her arms, the first time the little girl had moved at all since they'd left the house. She pushed the hair back from Betsy's ear, her little fingers sticky and warm on Betsy's cheek. She leaned in close, then whispered so quietly Betsy almost didn't hear it. When she finally made out what her sister had said, she turned slowly in the direction Esther was looking, and the little girl whispered it again.

"She's still here," she said. "She came with us."

Don't

Anna Minor-Weeks

His body has begun to stink.

I put him in the corner of the room. He is bigger than me, always bigger than me, and it took a while to get him shoved in the corner.

But there he is and there he stays.

I swept up the shattered glass of his beer bottle, mopped up the blood, and went back to living my life.

Pretending nothing is different, that nothing is wrong.

I pretend that there is not a corpse in the corner of the room.

Still, it feels like he is watching me.

It makes my skin crawl and I scratch, as though it was me rotting and festering, not him.

I try to avoid it, *avoid him*, but now that he is rotting, the stench is a constant reminder of what I've done.

The flawed illusion is cracking.

I don't know what to do.

"Don't leave this room, girl. Don't even think about leavin'."

I'm not supposed to leave the room.

The concrete is cold upon my feet as I pace in front of his body. I remind myself that his body is here but his soul is not.

Somehow, my pacing has strayed, and I end up standing up in front of the stairs.

I look at the door, his entrance and his exit. He would open the door and light would spill over into the dimness of my room. Then, he would step in, block the light with his darkness, and close the door.

I'm not allowed out of the room. I'm not allowed to go up the stairs.

The locks mock me.

He has the keys in his pocket. I know it. I could just take them out, walk up the stairs I'm not supposed to walk up, and unlock the door. It would be simple.

I step back. And look away from the stairs.

"You're not supposed to," he tells me. "You're not allowed."

Defiance, like joy, bubbles up in my heart. I walk up the stairs, quietly creeping.

Each step takes me further away from him and closer to freedom.

I run my fingers over the deadbolt locks and rest my hand on the doorknob. The smooth metal sphere feels good in my hand.

Fear strikes.

The outside world is scary, dangerous. That is what he always said. He would know. He lived up there. And if he is an example of someone from the outside world, maybe it is better to just stay here.

Stay down here like he told me to.

I run down the stairs. As I descend the stench crashes over me. Hell does not smell like fire and brimstone but of death and decay.

The next day, I cover my mouth and nose and approach his corpse.

His open eyes watch me, dull and dead, just as they were in life, as I steal from him.

I snatch the keys from his pocket, greedily, and backpedaled.

I walk up the stairs, fumble with the keys, and somehow manage to unlock the three locks.

The clicks are the most satisfying sounds I have ever heard. Better than the sickening crack as I hit him in the head.

I go to open the door but somehow find myself running down the stairs and back to the smell of decay.

I hold off escaping for as long as I can. I am not supposed to leave.

My stomach is painfully empty, and the water supply is beginning to dwindle, but it is the stench that gets to me.

Fear and hope choke me.

When it finally becomes unbearable I hear him hiss, "Don't," as I finally go back up the stairs I'm not allowed to go up and open the door I am not allowed to open and leave the room I'm not allowed to leave.

How the Horror Ends

Larissa Brown

))》◗ ● ◖ (((

"It's time to sleep, little one."

I take your hand and help you climb up into your high bed, and you scoot under your velvet blankets and white furs. The curtains around the bed whip with a twilight wind tonight, and the stone floors and walls are frigid.

"It's cold," I say. "Let's tuck all your hearts under the covers, and I'll tell you a story."

You pull the heavy blankets up over your vocal chords and settle in. Leaning over to kiss your cheek, I bump my head on the mobile we made out of paper and glue. The stars and moons and magic wands dance, wild. I take my place in the heavy wooden chair with the wings that seem to swallow my head—the only kind of chair we have in this castle—and shift around to get comfortable on the cushion. "All set?"

You nod, already sleepy.

"Ok, then." We're ready. "Once upon a time—"

"My nightlight!"

I sigh and go to the hearth to strike a match and light the night-candle in its iron frame. The familiar, flickering kitty-cat appears on the wall, its ears jumping and crackling with the flames.

"And a glass of water." You smile, my wicked girl.

"Silly," I say. "You can't drink water. Now, settle down."

Alright. We're ready, and I begin again. "The first time I lived, I was a queen, losing my mind with envy."

I'd recently married the king, who was handsome and absent. So, I sat around the castle and ordered the cooks to make me pies and jams. When I was not eating, I sat in a turret embroidering things with my stepdaughter, Snow. She was a delight, kind and generous, as well as stunning (and good at embroidery, of course). The more time I spent with her, the more decrepit I felt. Why could I not be as good and fair as she? Snow went about the castle grounds with her long pale skirts and dark braids, so winsome, and my desire turned into a sharp, bright jealousy.

One day, I couldn't take it anymore and was drowning my jealousy in a pie made of eels. Their bulging eyes stared up at me, and an idea struck. I ordered a huntsman to take Snow into the woods, stab her and bring me her lungs and liver. If I ate them, I would get her beauty! I did eat them (with salt and a touch of rosemary) and they were delicious, but nothing happened. I got no prettier or younger, and I still felt jealous.

The next time I lived, it was Snow's heart I demanded.

"You lived again?!"

"Come, little one. You know I have lived many times. Now, listen."

I lived again and again, sometimes demanding Snow's liver, sometimes her heart, sometimes eating it or sometimes saving it in a jeweled box. Each time was different except for two things: I always envied her, and I was never allowed to be her.

Soon, I became other queens, too. I became stepmothers and witches and kings. Over thousands of years, I entered into hundreds of bodies, and every time I envied innocent, refined, beautiful princesses. Darlings, treasures, with their symmetrical features and dewy skin. I wanted to be them, and so I ate them. (Well, some I hoarded in a drawer.)

I expanded my harvest to include other body parts. As king, I sent one of my men to bring me the hands of the virtuous and fair miller's daughter. (After all, the man could not pay his rent.) As a desperate, greedy mother, I forced my daughters to take a knife to their own clumsy toes so they would fit into a slipper of glass. (Who needs to walk when you're a queen, anyway?) I sheared off yards and yards of a princess's magic hair. I took a tongue, a voice, from a lithe little mermaid who wanted things she should not. I took organs. I took feet. I took the waking consciousness of at least one.

"You were really hungry," she interrupted

"Well, yes, but..."

I consumed, but not out of physical hunger. No, in the Great Halls of my many queendoms, there was plenty of mutton and pheasants and fish and those little dumplings with the ground meat and bread crumbs. (A great appetite was a virtue!)

No, I was not physically hungry. I was envy incarnate, and I wanted what those pretty girls had. If I owned her hands, I would become part miller's daughter, generous and kind. If I ate her organs, I would become part Snow, pure and fair beyond compare. If I consumed her consciousness, I would become part sleeping princess, serene and eternally youthful.

It did not work. I ate girls, and I did not feel lovelier, purer, wittier. I did not feel more courageous and generous. I stole hearts and livers and tongues, and nothing I ate made me feel worthy. (Honestly, I felt too full and disgusted with myself.) I was still envious, and not a single draught of blood down my throat could cool the burning of my own nature. I was still jealous, and nothing I ate could ever change that.

Nothing, that is, until I ate the handsome prince.

On a sweltering midsummer day, I was a girl walking down a dusty road toward a village. I was so heavy with jealousy that I stumbled as if drugged. My sister, the queen, had given birth to the most angelic little babes—three of them!—and she was now known even farther and wider for her exquisiteness and grace and fertility. I was left unknown, a dark figure in the shadows she threw.

I had an idea. When I reached the little town, I would nab three puppies, throw them in a sack and return to the castle where I would substitute the little dogs for my three perfect nieces. The pups would take the place of my sister's children, so I could steal the real babies and abandon them in the woods. When the king learned that his children were dogs, he would throw my sister in a tower at the very least, or perhaps put her to work doing menial labor.

Relishing the vision of my sister discovering her babies were gone, and of her being sent to trudge forever on a treadmill, I did not hear the prince approaching. He came riding up to me, rearing on his steed and showering me with dust.

"Are you in need, my lady?"

I laughed out loud. "Is it really that simple?"

He cocked his head in confusion like one of the puppies I was after.

"No," I said right away. What could this witless do-gooder do for me?

He swept his arm as if to bow while still seated on his horse. "I am off, then. I have heard of a princess locked in a castle keep. I seek her."

His silly feather bobbed in his cap as he rode away, and I wondered. Was I working too hard? Stooping to such extreme and ridiculous measures (stealing puppies, for goodness' sake) to become lovely?

I was so full of body parts I could burst, and the prince—good incarnate!—was able to get closer to all the princesses than I had ever managed to do. If only I could get that close instead of sending huntsmen and tax collectors to gather their parts, but never, sadly, their essences.

This puppy-seeking girl was bitter, and my envy was honed like a blade. I knew I could do whatever I wanted at that moment. I could take the prince, no problem, and when I ate him, I would shimmer with goodness, explode with it.

As the prince, I could get close enough to slip right into the arms of princesses. I would kiss them all, and I would suck the purity and beauty right out of their lungs instead of eating it or hiding it in a dresser drawer. I would finally soothe the eternal desperation that sat thick in my throat—

"Were you wearing a dress?"

"A dress? Well, yes, love. I was the young queen's sister. I had a fabulous dress! Long and blue with a golden belt. I ripped that dress as hard as I could, and I smeared it with dirt so it would look ragged."

"Like mine!"

"Yes, just like your dress. Now, close your sockets and try to sleep."

Looking back, it was not a great dress for prowling in a peasant village, but it was perfect for luring the prince. I called after him. "Wait!"

He turned back with another dramatic spray of dust. "Yes, my lady?"

"I do need your help. Please," I said pathetically. I made myself tremble and look afraid. "I am the queen's sister. A horrid man dragged me away from the castle. A huntsman. He wanted to cut out my lungs and have his way with me."

The prince jumped into action. He swooped down and lifted me with one arm, and I landed in the saddle before him. He was settling me into place and getting the horse turned around, and he did not expect it when I kicked the animal hard and made it dart into the woods. The prince was knocked off the saddle by a low-hanging branch, and as he held his head and mumbled his confusion, I took a kitchen knife from my belt, carved him up and ate him. He was so sweet going down! As soon as I finished licking his life's blood off my fingers (and burping to end the meal, of course), I fell into a deep sleep.

I woke with a dopey sense of wonder. I stared up into the trees with awe. I held up a hand, and it was strong and smooth and ready for action. I was happy and full of hope for another terrific day.

Was this what it felt like to be a prince?

I sat up and stretched my arms, and it was so satisfying! I was no longer stooped with cruelty. Strangest of all, I had no desire to steal those puppies anymore or to replace my nieces. I desired nothing more than to adorn the little ones with flower crowns and kiss their chubby feet. I felt the most curious absence. I was not jealous.

I leapt onto the magnificent horse and returned to the castle, and there I charmed the ladies and drank good ale before taking off to be a prince somewhere else.

I did this again and again, and they were all fine and wonderful lives.

I rode a swift white charger in the sunshine, finding maidens in need along the way like so many wildflowers to pick. I crossed streams. I climbed towers. I saw the sun set from atop a turret in brilliant shades of purple and gold. I held young women in my arms, and instead of tasting their insides, I tasted their lips. I kissed Snow, I kissed Sleeping Beauty, I kissed the princesses who had been turned to cats and birds. I kissed them all, and each time our lips met, curses flew off like scattered ravens, frogs leapt away, and poison apples rolled in the dust. My honorable body stirred with the most squeaky-clean lust it hardly deserved the word. (After all, we were no longer animals.)

Don't get me wrong. Hundreds of years ago princes, too, were warped and wicked, but those days were gone. I saved, I cherished. I married all, raped none. We lived happily ever after. In grand castles, we stood at stone window sills and sent our goodwill out over the land. I did good things for the people I once hurt, and they paid attention to me. They lavished me with all sorts of good things. Still, I always searched for the key to transforming into a princess.

As time went on, being good became tedious, and I tried to shake it up.

I became the jolly men who welcomed Snow White into their hut. I became a fairy godmother who dressed little Cinder in royal clothes. I loved every one of the girls and women. Snow with her intact organs. Beauty with her waking intelligence and wit. The miller's daughter with her hands cast of silver. The cat with its dainty feet. (I pet its soft white fur until it purred.)

But it was just one day after another of being helpful. Over and over, I helped maiden after maiden, never succeeding in absorbing their fairness, their ethereal loveliness, their precious, elegant gaits, and comely hands. I had, instead, a messy beard, and my princely tights chafed. I'd made a terrible mistake.

One day, I was loping around prince-ing, when I heard yet another cry for help from the woods. My steed and I dove into the trees to find the maiden in need. There she was, pink-cheeked, frilly-dressed, with a turned ankle.

"I was collecting mushrooms," she said. "And I tripped."

"Strange occupation for a maiden," I said, and I swept her into my arms and carried her to the edge of the woods.

"That makes sense," she said. "Because I am not a maiden. I am an omnipotent witch."

I dropped her on the ground, and I looked at my fingers as if they were burned. "A witch?!"

"Look," she said, righting herself and brushing off her skirts. "I am here to help you."

"Are you going to grant me a wish?"

"Haha," she said. "Very funny. No, I am here to tell you something of grave importance."

I struck a princely pose and waited.

"For thousands of lifetimes, you were envious. Now, you've been good and helpful"—did I hear a sneer in her voice?—"but you grow tired of it."

"How do you know that?"

"Come now, anyone can see." I looked down at myself and realized my tunic was smeared with gravy. I felt my head, and my feather was crooked.

The witch then told me something incredible. "You tried to become delicate and comely by eating princesses. Then, as the prince, by kissing them. But the real solution is so much simpler. All you have to do is stop trying."

She explained that if I just let go of being such a good prince, I would be able to retire and receive my reward.

Could it be that easy?

"If I just become bad at being a prince, I can stop, and I'll get everything I always wanted?"

"That's right," said the witch. "Everything you always wanted."

I imagined myself as Snow, finally, with my long dresses flowing behind me. As Cinder, with my dainty slippers. As that sad and lonely mermaid, silently combing her hair with an anemone, so enchantingly wistful and shiny.

I did not think about how the witch made no sense. Why would I get everything I'd always wanted just by being boring? By being bad at something? (But I was the prince, after all, not sharp enough to ask these kinds of questions.) And so I did as the witch said, and I became even duller than I already was. I went out into the world uninspired with no love for pursuing and overpowering evil. I felt no joy in scooping up maidens off the side of the road or climbing locked towers to release them.

I became less vigorous, ranged closer to home. I was no longer dashing or aggressive or resplendent. I moped around making goats' eyes at the princesses and carrying their little dogs for them. Children who listened, at bedtime, to the old tales about my princely prowess just rolled their eyes. They knew the princesses would be fine without me.

I lean over you, now, and whisper, "Are your lids closed, child?"

You don't respond, and I so carefully draw away so I will not wake you.

I could stop now, but I do not want to be left hanging as a fading, lazy prince. I speak to myself, oh so quietly. "I'll finish the story, anyway."

At last, I had become such a loser that I was finished. I had been hundreds of fine princes in the past, and now my work was done. This four-poster with its downy pillows and swirling white curtains would be my long-awaited deathbed.

"This exact bed?"

"You're not asleep?!" I sigh, thwarted. "Yes, this very bed."

That night, the witch's promise would come true. "You will get everything you always wanted."

I slept, drifting into memories of all the dashing, kissing, and plucking from danger that I'd accomplished. I dreamed of the many young women in their rags that turned into delicate gowns when I kissed them, their bedraggled hair turning to slender cones trailing long veils. I dreamed of my turn. *When I wake,* I thought, *I will be them!*

A shift in the room woke me. A presence, soft and sinister as curtains moving with no breeze. I felt—and heard—delicate things fluttering. Saw the indistinct shape of a girl, her hand pressed to the windowpane, looking at the moon and lawn. Was it her? The princess I would become? Finally, I would get to be made of courage, purity, and innocence. I would be fair and comely and have excellent posture and balance. I trembled with anticipation.

And yet, something was not right.

It might have been the billowing bed-curtains, but it looked to me like the girl at the window wore a ripped and ragged nightgown and something had spilled, like ink, like chocolate, down her dress. I could just make out the form of ponderous necklaces and the movement of wings beating where there might have been a corset. She was no princess.

"Who are you?"

With shaking hands, I lit my candle, and she emerged.

In the moonlight, I saw the stitches that held her skin together. In some places, she appeared blushing and radiant. In others, I could see through gaps in her skin into her insides where moist things oozed and pulsed. Human hearts—a dozen at least—hung on intricate brass chains around her neck. Each beat its own rhythm, a rapid chaos that made my own heart careen. Then, they beat once in unison. Then again, wild.

The heavy hearts swayed as she moved toward me. A few got tangled in her wet lungs, and they spasmed. Her throat gulped, but she could not find air because a rigid, slick organ was lodged there. A voice box? The root of a tongue wrapped around it, and the tip of the tongue stuck out between her skeletal teeth.

She reached for me with hands that looked like silver in the candlelight, but they were flesh. They were sewn roughly to her wrists with red ribbon, the ends dangling like streams of blood all the way to the floor. She came closer, and from under her tattered hems, I saw inhuman things. The feet of an animal. (It took me a moment to remember the cat.)

With the grace of pain, she sat on the edge of my bed and turned her face to me. She had no eyes. There was no story in which I had demanded them.

The girl reached a severed-and-sewn hand toward my face, and I clenched my eyes and braced for the creeping chill of her touch, but I was shocked. She was warm. Not the warmth of sunshine, but the wrong kind of warmth, like the rush of blood on a thigh, like wetting the bed. (Or had I actually done that in my terror?)

Then, those vocal chords vibrated. That tongue moved. "Mommy?"

Dread spilled into my chest and guts. All I could do was hold my covers up to my trembling chin.

She spoke again, and her voice was pure yearning. "I looked for you so long."

The girl laid down beside me, settled against me, and tears fell from the holes where eyes might have been. I held her, and my fingers slipped into her liver. A cacophony of beating and pulsing pushed against my chest. She shivered and asked with the voice of a mermaid, "Do you still want me?"

Her raw voice was familiar. It was how I once sounded, begging in the dark to be wanted. I felt the throat-stretching pain of being left behind.

Did I want her? Did I want this suck and release of lungs against my breasts? Too many hearts, each one a slippery, hot sphere against my ribs. Did I want to hold them and shake each one like a sick snow globe to reveal the castles and keeps where I once lived and breathed and ordered their harvest? Did I want this child whose liver slimed my fingers? This one who called me Mommy in a voice like desolate rocks above the sea. Her claws stretched and retracted against my shins. Did I want to stay here, forever pinned under the foulness of all the parts I demanded?

I held her tight.

"Yes," I said. "I do."

And power rushed in!

I held her, and a thousand years of doing good was released! I felt the swell of energy and the zing of glorious evil in my fingertips! I remembered the taste of each piece she was made of, and it did not feel acidic in my throat. My true nature felt like those delicious poison apples, so ripe and dangerous. How could I have wanted to become a princess? I was pure envy! The most powerful of all the forces, gleaming and glorious.

Now, I understood. Assembling my daughter, collecting part after part, was not driven by a desire to become all those princesses. It was driven by my own wickedness, by jealousy for its own burning sake. I was not absorbing good girls. I was feeding my own black heart.

We laid that way together, and I held her. I pulled the wool blanket up over her many hearts, and she fell asleep against me, a wonderfully wretched bundle of love, and my nightgown soaked up all that she seeped.

You are all I've ever wanted. I whispered against her foul hair. She was a vision, a jewel. She brought me back to myself.

Now, here tonight, I kiss the top of your lovely head once again, and I whisper the end of the tale.

"And that little girl was you."

Feet Back in Floodwater

Jaclyn Wilmoth

))))◐(((

own a side street *soi*, which itself was down another side street *soi*, which probably had no real name, Bassie had come to the only speck of light in the night. She worried that she might spook the house and send it scurrying off, taking with it the only light she could see, so she stood outside the gate and stared at it. She couldn't take her eyes off the chicken legs. They were long and slender, like the drumsticks of roosters she had only seen in Thailand. But these stems stood twice her height. The teak of the stilts was carved into intricate feathers, which were so detailed that they ruffled as the breeze blew past. The thighs tapered down into skinny shins, which were covered with scales. The claws were sunken in the black water, but Bassie was sure they were there, grasping at the ground beneath them. On top of the teak-stilt drumsticks stood a house.

Like those of the house, Bassie's feet were submerged in water. It nearly came up to the edge of her galoshes and it stank. Years of Bangkok's sewage swam around her shins, and she could almost feel the water monitors and Burmese pythons wrapping around her submerged ankles. The water itself seemed darker than the night, as if it emanated blackness. The air was still dense with Bangkok's light pollution, though the city was dark and silent. Evacuated. The electricity had been out for days.

She had been sent out to get candles the day before, so her stepmother and stepsisters had spent a whole night in the dark already, stranded on the island of their home. They refused to go out in the floodwaters, preferring instead to be encased in white tiles and walls.

Even before the flood, they never liked to leave. Bassie had offered to go find candles, needing the break from that house. She had not realized that most of the city was empty. She'd already spent nearly twenty-four hours knocking on doors, sloshing through the rising water, and looking for light.

The house before her looked in some ways like a traditional Thai-style house, carved out of water-resistant teak wood and propped up where the water couldn't reach it, designed in a time when Bangkok remembered that every year the rains brought floods, and the floods were welcomed because they made the rice grow. But now, the jungle had been poured over with concrete so that towering trees became skyscrapers, and when the floods came, the water just sat. Bodhi trees and strangler figs, remnants of the rainforest beneath the city, refused to give in and pushed their way up through cracks in the concrete, dripping heart-shaped leaves on the sidewalks. This house was, however, very definitely not traditional. Old-style Thai houses did not have long, too-skinny chicken legs.

Bassie sighed and shook her head, cursing her stepmother. She had no choice but to suck it up and ask for help from whoever lived in this house-ready-to-run. Ever since moving to Bangkok, Bassie felt as if she'd been living in some alternate reality that was so close to the sun that things stopped making sense. Everything was slightly blurred by the heat so that nothing was solid. She was not sure if the place itself was scrambled or if her brain was being fried, but this breakfast was hard to swallow.

Were those bones? Bassie walked closer to the gate but hesitated to touch it. The off-white posts of the fence were arranged perfectly parallel to each other, and yet, they were amiss, slightly different sizes. She took a deep breath and slid the gate to the side. It rolled easily on its tracks—for about a foot. It stopped there, as if trying to deter her. She squeezed herself through the narrow opening.

The house had one singular window. The light glowing from inside said there must be someone home. She walked up the steps to the front door. The edges of the doorframe were pointed into fangs, as if a snake beckoned her into its belly. She reached into her pocket and fingered its contents, asking for help. Courage enough. She knocked.

"Aren't you a little old to be playing with dolls?"

Bassie had not even seen the door open, shocked as she was by the figure before her. The woman was hunched so that she nearly folded in half. Her face was so wrinkled as to be almost inhuman. Her hair was long and white, scraggly gossamer cobwebs that swept the floor. She was squat and rounded, her skirts making a small dome, and Bassie wondered what she hid beneath.

"It's from my mother," Bassie replied.

"The question still stands." The old woman squinted, taking stock of Bassie. Given the decrepitude of the woman's body, Bassie was surprised that she could see her well enough to know Bassie was a foreigner.

Bassie squinted back and scrunched her freckled nose. The old woman's eyes on her made Bassie aware of her body. Bassie's raven hair contrasted sharply with the ashen, wiry hair of the woman who had answered her knock. She was nearly as short as the folded old woman. Bassie was the spitting image of her mother, which sometimes made her father not want to look at her. She wondered even if this was why he spent so much time away from home "on business."

"Do you have any candles?" Bassie asked.

"Hmmf." The woman turned around and shuffled back into her house, leaving the mouth of the door gaping open. Bassie hesitated. The tiny wooden doll in her pocket urged her on, and she followed into the house.

It was incredibly small and very hot. Even in November, Bangkok was steaming. And with the floodwaters below, steaming was not an exaggeration. The air seemed as if it also was flooded, so thick that Bassie felt like she was floating. On the far side of the one-room house, there was a fireplace with a fire going strong. It wasn't often that houses in Bangkok were hotter inside than it was outside. Next to the chimney stood a giant ceramic mortar and pestle. The shutters of the house were closed, and there was no ventilation, yet the woman did not sweat.

"What will you give me for it?"

"Excuse me?" Bassie replied, widening her eyes innocently and trying her sweetest Thai-style intonation. Her stepmother's errand was already more of an ordeal than she had expected, but everything in this city was like that.

"You expect me just to give you candles and fire in this situation? They are needed by everyone."

Bassie's eyes settled on the fireplace.

"You must help an old, poor woman like me. My eyes are not good. Can you sort this rice?"

Bassie tried not to give a look of incredulity. Everyone she knew in Bangkok bought pre-sorted, processed rice. It was a modern city; there weren't rice paddies downtown. Also, Bassie was sure that this woman's eyesight was just fine if she could make out Bassie's blue, foreign eyes in the darkness and know to speak English to her.

"I don't know how to do that. I really just need to get home."

"Without any light?"

The old woman had her there. Bassie imagined returning to the cold, white house of her stepmother without having anything to show for her time away.

The old woman nodded toward the bin of rice. "Just take out the stones and dark grains. And then you can cook it."

"All of it?" There must have been five kilos of rice there. Bassie scanned the room for a stove. She had never cooked over a fire, and she was honestly not good at cooking rice. When Thai people asked her if she ate rice or bread, she always answered bread without hesitating. Not that she knew how to bake bread, either. But god, was she tired of white rice.

"It's a flood," the old woman said. "Who knows when I'll be able to cook again." She dragged the giant mortar and pestle out the front door. She turned around. "Treat it gently. You have to coax it to cook until it's soft and plump and white. Rice is a shy, young girl. You can't force her."

The woman smiled and her wrinkles softened. In the first graceful move she had made, her hips rocked through the threshold. The mouth of the door yawned slowly open then snapped shut behind her.

With the door and window closed, the house started to sweat. Bassie dipped her hand into the uncooked rice, listening to the rain sound it made as it fell through her fingers. She thought back to all the times her stepmother had cooked rice since they had moved to Thailand. Plain white rice. Like eating wet Styrofoam.

Bassie took the little wooden doll out of her pocket. The carving never seemed to wear. At times like this, when surroundings were confusing and unfamiliar, this small memento of her mother was comforting. She set the doll into the rice and sat on the floor. She leaned over the bin, and tears started to fall, collecting in the dryness of the raw rice.

"Everything's a chore," she said to the doll. "Nothing is simple here."

She had been awake and walking through the city for more than a day. It had seemed like such a small endeavor to find some candles, and now Bassie wondered at what the point was. Surely darkness was easier than all this. The heat of the still Bangkok night combined with the fire weighed her head so that it drooped to the side. Her eyelids were not far behind. She let the swelter win, and her childhood rushed in.

She stood in the warm sun of her homeland. The day was beautiful, and she was dressed like a tiny princess, but there was an uneasiness in the billowy clouds above. Her father smiled, his gentle crow's feet twinkling at the corners of his eyes. It was one of the first times he'd smiled since her mother's death.

The brightness of the sunshine washed everything white: Bassie's pink dress, the cream dress of her new stepmother, the baby blue sky. It all glowed like an overexposed photograph. The day was too bright for comfort. Perhaps her father's smile was only squinting. The flowers were all bleached.

Bassie stood alongside her two new sisters, who sparkled in diamonds and pearls, dazzling like teeth. She was afraid to look at them.

But she could not take her eyes off her father and her new stepmother. He dressed in black, calming, soothing, and basking in the sun. He winked at Bassie and spoke words that evaporated before she could hear them. Then he smiled at this new stepmother.

The frostiness of her stepmother's dress seemed to be absorbing the warmth of the sun, soaking up the summer so that the day turned brisk. Bassie's world was getting brighter and more arctic. Blazingly pallid and corpse-like. Alabaster butterflies danced in the wind like cremation ashes. Wisps of dandelions could no longer hold on to their stems in the chill. They swirled in the drafts of sunlit air like snowflakes.

Bassie looked again to her father. The warmth in his eyes, his smile seemed to harden. His face froze into a mask.

When Bassie woke, she was covered with a gentle sweat. Cinders from the fire and tendrils of steam from the freshly cooked rice fluttered around the wooden doll as the door opened. The woman burst into the room faster than anyone her age should be able to move.

Behind the woman, the hue of the sky was changing, contrasting more and more with the black water. The sun and the water rose. Just past the front gate, a pale elephant splashed through the flood, moving clumsily like a bulky, round toddler. Bassie had seen white elephants in statues and paintings but never in person. They were sacred in Thailand, the animal that gave the Buddha's mother a lotus before he was born, and a symbol of purity and status.

Traditionally, these albino elephants were not allowed to be put to work. It was said that Thai kings used to give white elephants to

people they wanted to be rid of, gifting them a large animal to feed and
house which they could not use for any practical purpose. It was no
longer legal to have elephants in the city, but it still happened often
enough. Apparently, traditions and laws went out the window as the
city shut down. The *mahout*, who rode the elephant, was easy to see,
dressed all in white, like a Buddhist nun or a child ready for first
Communion. The water was up to the knees of the elephant. Bassie's
galoshes would be useless now.

As she wondered about the best way to get home, the door slid
shut. The relatively cool breeze of the outside air was cut off, as was
the sweet smell of jasmine mixed with sewage. It was replaced in her
nostrils by burning wood. Even the closed door was a barrier stronger
than the pull of her stepmother's home.

"Finished?" the woman asked, eyeing Bassie.

Bassie quickly picked up her wooden doll and shoved it in her
pocket. Her face hardened as she nodded.

"More to you than meets the eye, eh, girl?" Her voice was high
and scratchy. It put Bassie on edge. The woman looked younger in this
light, where the shadows didn't accentuate her wrinkles.

"May I have the candles now?"

"That easily?" The woman looked at her knowingly. "You hardly
did anything." She nearly smiled. Her face contorted into a scowl, and
at the same time, her features softened. She must be older than anyone
Bassie had ever met. And yet, there was a beauty about her. Something
enthralling and alluring. Her eyes were lined with charcoal and the way
that she squinted made Bassie both uncomfortable and titillated.

The woman scooped a bit of rice into a bowl and handed it to
Bassie, who cupped the bowl as if she were trying not to touch it. She
hesitated. The old woman wrapped her hands around the bowl and
pushed it against Bassie's belly.

"Thank you," Bassie said, her voice caught in her throat. The
woman gave her no utensils. Bassie scooped a bit up into her fingers
and brought them to her mouth. The woman raised an eyebrow and
sighed.

Bassie was surprised at the taste of the grains as they touched
her tongue. The rice tasted of the earth, of sunshine and dirt, of the
wetness of paddies. It burst as she chewed it. It was ripe and lush,
pregnant with the potential of wind and rain. The silt of centuries of
floods rushed over her taste buds. It was lushly chartreuse, zipping of
the first shoots of life.

"Do you have a name?" Bassie asked.

"You may call me Baba."

Bassie looked back at her bowl then shyly to the woman, wondering what was happening to her. She was not sure she could endure another bite that gushed like that. But she couldn't hold herself back. The corners of Baba's mouth sparkled and egged her on. The old woman put her fingers to her own lips in anticipation. Bassie took another pinch of rice. Hours passed as she ate a few morsels at a time, and each one filled her mouth with the pubescent seeds of cities, the possibility of building civilizations.

After only a bit, Bassie felt full. She yawned.

"You must be feeling very sleepy after all the work you did last night, dear." Baba raised her eyebrow and moved closer, touching her wrinkled fingers to Bassie's hair. She stood taller, meeting Bassie's eyes with a questioning, inviting brow. Bassie found it difficult to look away.

"I am, but I should be getting home," Bassie blurted, trying to keep her eyes open.

Baba didn't respond but held Bassie's gaze.

"May I have the candles now?" Bassie shifted her weight.

"You've not done enough to earn my fire yet, girl," Baba answered. "But I will give you another task."

"Another one?"

"Or I could eat you," Baba answered. She did not smile. She stroked Bassie's chin.

Bassie could hardly keep her head up. "It's so hot in here," she said.

"I need chili paste to go with the rice." Baba brought out the mortar and pestle. The mortar was large enough for a person to fit inside it, and the pestle would clearly take two hands to move. *Or I could eat you.* Baba opened the door to a small closet, which held a store of chilies, garlic, and onions piled on the floor. Some of the onions rolled to her feet. Bassie gave the woman an annoyed look.

"Keep your sass in check, girl, and make sure you make it plenty spicy. The paste should be hot and fiery on my tongue. I'll be back." As Baba opened the door, the midday light filled the room. It was stiflingly hot. The floodwaters oozed the brackish green of sewers and rushed higher, climbing the steps to Baba's house. The air filled with the smell of Bangkok's *klongs*, black canals that ran past malls and corrugated metal shanty towns, soaking up everything the city excreted. Bassie couldn't stomach the idea of wading or swimming home in that.

In the daylight, she could better see the gate that surrounded Baba's. Thighbones, shins, and arm bones made the posts, while collarbones held them together lengthwise. Every few meters, a skull was placed on a raised shoulder blade. The eye sockets glowed in the noontime sun as if alive. The bones were orderly, forming an intricate embellishment that stretched all around the house. Bassie pictured Baba standing on a pile of bones, skulls in her hands, dancing a primal ritual of death and creation as she built the fence. Her arms flailed as if she had ten of them, and her eyes glowed a savage red. And Bassie was alongside Baba, weaving with her a shining mandala, a protective reminder of the circle of creation and destruction, all made of human bodies.

This was too much for Bassie. She made her way slowly down the steps of Baba's house. Most of them were underwater. She went in to the top of her galoshes, realizing that there were still four more steps to go. The water was nearly up to her neck and surged, rushing quickly to the south. There was a splash at her ankles, the darkish green of the water lapped at her thighs. Pushing out of the flood was a water monitor, its forked tongue licked her legs as its claws wrapped around her. Bassie ran up the stairs and back to the safety of the belly of the house, slamming the door behind her.

Inside, Bassie tentatively approached the mortar and pestle. She touched the ring of the mortar. There was something comforting about the roundness of it. The way that it curved was inviting and Bassie nestled herself into its concave cradle. And here she was: motherless, alone, a hemisphere away from her birth, in the middle of a natural disaster.

She took the doll out of her pocket and gently ran her fingers over it. It was short and voluptuous, wood made soft by the hourglass contours. It was so small and round that it was barely recognizable as human-shaped, and yet it echoed memories of her mother perfectly. Bassie fell asleep clutching the doll in the embrace of the mortar.

Cuddled by the warmth of her childhood home, which was cuddled by the coziness of the forest, Bassie burrowed into her mother's lap. There were fireflies all around dancing in pairs, starry eyes keeping watch over her. Embers from the fireplace floated in the air and congregated in Bassie's hair and on her mother's chest. Her father watched them from across the room and worry wrought his face.

Her mother coughed and reached under the blanket. As the wind blew, the trees outside held hands and danced in a circle around the house.

Bassie wanted to join, but she wouldn't leave her mother's lap. The wind sang a song and used their small house as a drum.

"Kvass, please," her mother said.

Bassie's father hesitated before making his way to the kitchen. As he left, the fire was emboldened. Flames illuminated the room. The light frolicked on the floor, on the ceiling, on Bassie and her mother. The walls smiled. Autumn leaves looked into the window, asking to enter. They pressed their fiery faces to the glass, waiting eagerly to see what would unfold inside. The fireflies and embers pirouetted together, unsure of who was flying and who was falling.

"This is for you." Her mother opened her hand to reveal a small wooden doll. Its features were finely carved: flowing wooden hair, softly draped wooden skirt. Two of the fireflies came to land on the doll's face, setting her eyes aglow, and the doll's lips parted as it sighed.

"Ask her for help when you need it, Bassie, but don't forget to feed her. She will be everything you will ever need." Her mother coughed again. The fire coddled them in its blanket. Bassie hugged the doll under her chin and fell asleep.

In Baba's house, Bassie woke up next to the fire and had trouble seeing straight. The room was suffocatingly hot. Her hair stuck to her face and neck. The door was open, but Bassie was alone. The fresh air was too apprehensive to enter, so she had to track it down herself.

She sat on the front steps, an enticing snack framed by the mouth of the door, and wondered if she could coax the house into running away with her. She could sit on these steps while the chicken legs picked up and ran out of the flooded, steaming metropolis into some idyllic rainforest. She could be alone, running naked through banana trees and orchids. No stepmother, no stepsisters, no chores. Just singing mangoes and cicadas.

She thought of lost pasts and lost futures. She tried to remember what it felt like to be home. It was gone now. The house she grew up in, the land she grew up on, they were no longer hers. The people who had made her feel at home were no longer hers. Even the dreams she'd had of traveling and making homesteads in foreign lands had evaporated. She felt adrift in the floodwaters. A compass was useless because there was no direction toward which she could travel. She could not go back, nor could she move forward.

In the distance, flood waters splashed. With glazed eyes, Bassie looked in the direction of the sound, taking very little notice of the elephant and rider passing in front of the gate. The animal was a pinkish red, the color of clay. Its backside swayed and bewitched. The scarlet *mahout* stared at Bassie, but she was too deep in the rainforest to meet the gaze.

"Finished already, eh?" Baba appeared on the steps as if out of nowhere, dry and fresh. Her hair seemed to glow in the light. Her eyes and lips looked fiery.

Bassie tried to peel her hair off her skin. She felt unkempt and self-conscious next to Baba.

"Where's the chili paste?" Baba asked.

Bassie didn't answer, and Baba pushed past her into the house. Bassie followed.

The mortar held a sticky, red chili paste that stuck to the sides of it as if clinging to a lover. Bassie's doll rested between the mortar and the pestle. As Bassie rushed to stuff it in her pocket, Baba raised an eyebrow.

"Give me your hands," she said.

"What?"

Baba grabbed both Bassie's hands by the wrists and lifted them to her face. She eyed them carefully and then touched Bassie's fingertips to her tongue, slowly, suspiciously. Her mouth was warm and smooth. She took one finger into her mouth and sucked.

"Clean," she said. "You haven't touched a chili."

Bassie pulled her hands away. "I used the pestle."

"To separate the tops? To cut the chilies and the onions?" Baba said. "I'm on to you, girl."

The woman scooped paste out of the mortar with her finger and touched it to her lips without opening her mouth. It turned her lips crimson and her cheeks followed suit. Her eyes gleamed as if a switch had been turned on inside her. With another scoop, she reached her fingers to Bassie's lips, applying the same fiery lipstick to Bassie's confused mouth. There was a rush of heat, from her lips to her face, and washing down through her body. Bassie licked her lips, and the flames inside her seemed to make the heat of the fire-lit tropical house more bearable. Droplets of sweat traced the contours of her body, and Baba followed each trail with her eyes. The heat rushed to Bassie's head and she closed her eyes as if she'd been caressed for the first time.

As Baba smiled at Bassie, she glowed that light of women who are pregnant or in love. Her hair was thick, curly, and bright, flames licking around her face, illuminating her crevasses so that there were no shadows. Baba ran her fingers over Bassie's jaw line, and Bassie's skin tingled.

"This will do," Baba said. Baba offered her more chili paste, and she took it eagerly, hot for Baba's approval. They fed each other gently as the sun began to set.

The fire was dwindling and the room was sticky. Rain started to beat against the roof, and Baba got up to open the door, hips swaying as she went. The rains had traveled down from the Himalayas to cool Bassie's skin and left small mountains of gooseflesh on her arms. Tiny Everests poked out from beneath her shirt. Baba didn't turn to look as Bassie walked up behind her. Instead, she kept her eyes out into the night. Passing in front of the boney gate was the darkened silhouette of an elephant and its rider, moving easily and deliberately through the water, as if they had slowed to look at Baba and her hungry house.

"They pass every day," Baba said to the rain. "They always pass."

Mahout and beast continued to lumber past, softly churning the floodwaters as they moved. The city was silent, and Bassie could hear the small tsunamis that the footsteps of the pachyderm sent toward the chicken-leg island where she stood. The eerie glow of millions of lights that had been turned off days ago still hung in the air, particles of light pollution held in place by the humidity, caught and magnified by rain that fell and didn't fall. The tiny light droplets backlit the *mahout* and the elephant, silhouetting them as one imposing, blackened animal. Bassie reached for Baba's hand, and Baba returned her grasp.

"There's one more thing I want you to do for me, and then you may have my fire."

Bassie did not object and Baba led her back into the house. The sultry heat of the room rushed to envelop her, tousling her hair. The elder climbed up on a chair and reached for a sack on a high shelf. As she reached, her body unfolded, revealing breasts, hips, an hourglass waist. She threw her head and shoulders back as she grasped the sack, and she looked strong, young. Bassie expected her to crinkle back into the rotund, enfeebled crone who first opened the door to her the night before, but she didn't. Bassie pulled herself straighter, trying to stand as tall as Baba, whose hair no longer touched the ground. Bassie thought she saw herself in the old woman.

Baba put the sack on the floor and opened it. Tiny black teardrops spilled out, crawling and writhing out of the bag like ants.

"Sesame seeds," Baba said, as Bassie recoiled. "Nothing more. They need to be cleaned." Baba handed her a small cloth. "One by one."

Bassie nodded and dropped to her knees. The heat in the room lulled her eyelids together as if they were lovers on a torrid night. Her head drooped. She begged not to fall asleep while Baba was at her back. She straightened her shoulders and pulled herself awake. In her pocket, the doll stirred.

Baba rested a hand in Bassie's hair. "There, there," Baba said, and Bassie could hold on to wakefulness no longer.

It was a hot, obsidian night, the kind of black that glowed with the reflection of the lights around it. From inside the taxi, a young Bassie stared mesmerized and spellbound. City lights shone from convenience stores, from motorbike headlights, from the tiny bulbs of street carts. A family of five passed on a motorcycle, baby sandwiched between parents and toddlers grasping handlebars and mother's back. A leathery woman wove orchids into wreaths, and the scent shot through the windows and air conditioning of the car, smacking Bassie in the face. A man cycled past with a plastic display case instead of a little basket in front of his handlebars. As Bassie peered into the case, she saw a display of crickets, cockroaches, and beetles, all spiced and sautéed for sale. The sights and smells were cramped in, pushed up against the nudging shoulders of the taxi by the concrete walls that grew up on all sides. How could this place ever be home?

Together in the backseat with Bassie, her stepsisters slept. The metropolitan lights hung heavy in the air, blurred and refracted through the thick, tropical heat. The lights left trails behind them, as if the whole city were a nighttime photograph taken from a shaky tripod. The glares fluttered and flew in the air. The gaping mouths of her stepsisters yawned, inhaling and exhaling the night. They sucked in the glow of the street vendors and shops, swallowing Seven-Eleven signs and tiny bulbs hanging from extension cords attached to stalls. In the front, seat her stepmother, face of stone and determination, seemed to push the taxi on.

As the green and yellow cab moved further down the soi, *the road became narrower and more packed. There were no other cars anymore, only stalls and motorbikes, pedestrians as wide as the alley itself. The taxi nudged past all of them, none of whom noticed or acknowledged the car in the road. In front of the taxi, the city glared with the lights of commerce. Her sleeping sisters sucked them up one by one: the lights of the noodle soup stalls, headlights of motorbikes, blue TV light from inside evening homes. Her sisters' snores inhaled them all, swallowing them into the darkness of their stomachs. In the wake of their traversing was left only blackness, black eyes, black air, black street, black hair, black buildings, black stares.*

When Bassie awoke, Baba was sitting next to the fire, arms crossed into a pretzel over her chest. Her skirts were pulled up to her knees, which poked out shapely and full from beneath.

"I saw the whole thing, darling."

Bassie was still pulling herself out of her dream back into Baba's chicken-thigh cabin. Baba motioned toward the shining pile of black sesame seeds. On top of the newly cleaned pile sat Bassie's most prized possession, her little wooden doll. Its eyes glowed and it quivered.

"I knew there was more to you. You are destined for greater things."

Bassie shivered and stayed quiet.

"You can always count on natural disasters to bring fate to the forefront. When the earth starts to rumble and the waters get angry, it only means that something is amiss and needs to be set right. And here you are."

Baba rose from her chair. When she stood straight, Bassie admired the curve of her hips and breasts, the wave of her waist. Her hair had darkened to a flaming black, making an ebony halo around her face. Her skin glowed so that Bassie wondered if she would be hot to the touch, and she reached out a hand to her. As she brushed her arm, she felt a buzz; static sparks radiated from the contact.

"Eat, dear. You deserve it." Baba handed Bassie a bowl full of the rice, chili paste, and sesame seeds that Bassie's doll had prepared. The flavor was more than the sum of the ingredients. The rice burst with the fertility of seeds. The chili paste burned with the zest of passion. The sesame seeds brought them together in a deep, mature richness that filled every corner of Bassie's mouth. Baba ate too, and together they became giddy on the fullness of the meal. Bassie moved closer, resting her head on Baba's chest. Baba enveloped the whole of her body as if her arms were wings enclosing around her.

"You've earned my fire," Baba told her. In an overturned skull, she placed a candle and lit it with the fire from her hearth. As the flame on the wick grew, the fireplace darkened, leaving only embers.

"It's time for us both to go home," Baba sighed. "I'm so glad you've come."

Bassie pulled away from Baba's embrace and laid herself on the wooden table behind her, inviting Baba to follow. She did. Hips and thighs and the curves of bellies, collarbones, jawbones, and spines all mixed together on the table. Bassie latched on to Baba and buried into her. She gulped all she could from Baba, and Baba did the same, creating a spiraling mix of nectars through their bodies. Baba dined on toes and breasts and gasps, and Bassie nibbled elbows and buttocks and sighs. They gorged and swallowed until they had their fill.

Or I could eat you.

On the pile of rice, chili paste, and sesame, the eyes of Bassie's doll glimmered like glowworms, and it rattled in a way that it never had before. It seemed to have a wind about it, some intangible movement that held the air surrounding it. With the gentleness and ease with which things fall apart, it broke perfectly in two.

The hewn grandmother gave way to a seductive, passionate woman, who in turn gave way to a shy, misplaced girl. It was a doll within a doll, which broke again and again. Like the outside, the inside layers were not painted, but delicately carved. The smooth features of an array of beauties were etched into solid wood. Outwardly, she was a grandmother, large and portly, all encompassing. But within her, there existed ever-smaller selves until, at her core, she was a mere babe. She held within her generations yet to burst forth, versions of herself yet to be fleshed out. The dolls danced past Bassie and Baba, caressing their bellies and cheeks until they fell asleep.

On the pile of limbs and flesh, the doll broke open fully. Inside was the smallest, most unbreakable piece of all, a tiny house standing on chicken legs.

When Bassie awoke, she was alone. The flame in the skull continued to burn in the corner of the room, and the embers of the hearth had dimmed. The sky was just starting to fade. Bassie stood at the bottom of the steps, feet back in floodwater but this time without galoshes. The water had started to recede. In the twilight, she could see the reflection of her own glow. Her hair had grown, reaching almost to the water, and it was a shock of white that framed her face. She waded home, though empty streets and *sois*. She passed water monitors and pythons and looked them in the eye. They held her gaze and watched her march. Mango trees dropped their fruit in her hands. Even skyscrapers paid attention as she glided by.

When she reached her house, it was empty. Her stepmother and stepsisters gone, fled from the flood. She checked her room and the kitchen for some note, some forwarding address and found none. They had left her alone, far from the city of her birth, abandoned in a flood. Exhausted, she melted onto her bed and dreamed every dream she had ever known simultaneously.

She was sticky and hot, not just Bangkok hot, but something more. It was bright in her room. And smoky. The lines around her blurred and swirled and crackled. A fire raged around the skull that held her candle. She moved closer to it, and it lapped at her feet. She reached for the skull, and her hands cupped the flames, comforted, warmed. She brought the skull out of the house and stood in the waters. Turtles and river crabs came to sit beside her. She watched until the sky started to glow and splashing noises behind her pulled her out of her trance. A *mahout* rode a white elephant past, and Bassie wondered if it was the same one from the start of her journey. The *mahout* had hips that swayed with the elephant's stride. She was dressed in white cotton gauze, like a Buddhist nun, but the cuffs of her sleeves and pants were trimmed with silver beads. They tinkled as the rider passed. Her face and head were covered with the flowing cotton. She nodded to Bassie and a lock of glowing black hair fell from her headscarf.

Bassie knew she had only one place to go, and that it would be empty when she got there. She took her still-lit skull and started the procession back to where she'd been. The door of the house gaped open wide, inviting her inside. The snake mouth seemed to smile as she entered. Baba was gone and Bassie knew she would not be back. The rooster legs of the house twitched, ready to take Bassie anywhere she pleased. Her *matryoshka* doll sat on the mantle, whole and sealed shut. Its eyes glowed like embers of a fire from within its belly. She was home.

Scairy Tales for Modern Maidens

Emily Finhill

))) (((((

THE WOODS

There was once a dark wood where the animals' eyes were black as buttons, and the villagers whispered that monsters lurked in the shadows of the twisted trees. In the woods lived a girl and her father. The man was very poor, and though he loved his daughter as best he could, he couldn't scrape together enough food for both of them. Winter came to the dark forest, and the man knew that he and his daughter would starve if he didn't soon act.

So he said to his daughter, "I must go to town so the winter does not kill us both. If anyone comes to the door, don't open it unless they know the answer to our riddle."

The riddle was a secret between the father and the daughter, and no one else knew it. She agreed that she would not let anyone in. Her father brought in wood for the fire, set a jar of milk and a slice of bread on the table, and kissed his daughter goodbye. The girl bolted the door after her father, stoked the fire, drank the milk, and then sat down to spin yarn from sheep's wool.

The first night, there came a tapping on the cottage door just as the clock struck ten.

"Who is it?" the girl called.

"It's your father," replied a voice, and the voice sounded like her father.

"What is never full, no matter how much it's fed?"

"My belly," the voice replied, a hungry gurgle belying the father's voice.

"Wrong!" cried the girl, clutching her spinning in fear, for it was not her father. "Go away! I shall not open the door!"

Then, a mighty beating and shaking began that rocked the cottage on its foundation, and the beast roared with a growl that made the hair stand up on the girl's arms. She knew the monster wanted to tear her flesh from her bones with its sharp teeth and devour her. She mustered all her courage and screamed.

"Begone! I will never let you in!"

The cottage stilled. The night quieted. The girl went back to spinning.

The next day, the girl tended the fire and ate the bread and spun the wool. When her spinning was done, she began to wind the yarn. She wanted to see if her father was coming, but she dared not open the door.

That night, she sat winding yarn. As the clock struck ten, there was a knocking at the door.

"Who is it?" the girl called.

"It's your father," replied her father's voice. "Let me in, I'm cold and hungry."

"What is never full, no matter how much it's fed?" the girl asked.

"A wishing well," the voice replied with a hollow echo beneath the father's voice.

"Wrong," said the girl. "Go away, monster. You are not my father."

This time a mighty shrieking, like the shrieking of a hundred winter winds, rose up outside her door. It wailed around the house, shaking the windows and rattling the jambs. The girl shivered, for she knew the monster wanted to crack her bones apart with its strong claws and suck out the marrow. The girl stuffed yarn into her ears and screamed into the wind.

"Begone! I will never let you in!"

The wind stopped. The house stilled. All returned to peace and quiet.

The next day, the bread was gone. The girl tended the fire and wound her yarn. She was hungry and wanted to look for food, but she dared not open the door. She finished winding her yarn into balls and took out her needles to begin knitting. She knit and knit through the day.

She sat knitting into the night. When the clock struck ten, a knock came at the door again.

"What is never full, no matter how much it's fed?" she called.

"Please let me in," said a child's voice, full of fear. "I'm alone out here, and there are monsters!"

The girl grasped her knitting needles tightly. "I cannot let you in."

"Please, please, I'm afraid!" the child cried.

"I cannot open the door for anyone but my father," the girl said.

"But there are monsters out here that will surely devour me!"

The girl wept into her knitting, for she was afraid and did not know what to do.

"Begone!" she sobbed. "I will never let you in!"

All was quiet, except for a soft sobbing on the other side of the door. The girl put down her knitting and went to the door, for surely a beast wouldn't cry. She lifted the beam and was about to open the door when the sobbing turned to laughter. Cackling filled the cottage and long-taloned fingers reached through the crack in the door. The girl stabbed the claws with her knitting needles, and the laughter turned to screeching, and the paw retracted. She shoved the door closed and slammed the beam back in the lock. She spent the night curled in the center of the floor, sobbing with hunger and fear.

The next day, the girl was dizzy with hunger and aching with cold. There was no more wood, no more milk, and no more bread. Still, she knit and knit, for it was all she could do.

At ten o'clock that night, there was a knock at the door.

"What is never full, no matter how much it's fed?" the girl called.

"Your father is never coming back," a voice whispered through a crack in the door. "He left you alone to starve. Why not open the door and be done with it?"

"Go away. I shall not open the door."

The whispers filled the cottage, slivers of doubt and faithless thoughts invading every corner of the once-cozy home. It shook the foundations of the girl's heart, and rattled at the edges of her mind, for she knew that once she gave in, the monster would drink her blood like wine.

"Begone," the girl said weakly, her voice barely strong enough to speak. "I will never let you in."

The whispers stopped, and the insidious doubt retracted, and the girl was left alone in her cold cottage.

The next day, the girl didn't have the strength to move from her bed. She finished her knitting. She was so cold. She slept.

At ten o'clock, a knock came at the door. The girl was ready.

"What is never full, no matter how much it's fed?"

"A father's heart," replied her father's voice.

"Wrong," the girl whispered. "Do you want to know the answer, monster?"

"Yes," the monster snarled.

"If I tell you the answer, you have to give it to me," the girl said.

"And if I give it to you, will you let me in?"

"I swear it."

"Then we have a bond. Tell me what is never full, no matter how much it is fed."

"The answer is fire," the girl said.

"Very well." The monster roared, and soon fingers of flame licked at the bottom of the door. The girl flung open the door and saw that the monster had set the little cottage ablaze. It was a fearsome monster, eight feet tall with wings on its back, horns on its head, and the feet of an eagle.

"And now, girl, I am going to eat you." The monster lunged towards her.

The girl struck hard, driving her knitting needle into one of the beast's golden eyes. The monster slumped forward, bleeding black blood, hungry mouth still gaping open and empty.

"No, monster," the girl whispered. "I am going to eat you."

And the girl roasted the monster who had tried to devour her over the burning embers of the home that had become a prison. She tore the beastflesh from the fearsome bones with her sharp teeth and cracked its bones apart with her strong hands and sucked out the marrow and drank its blood like fine wine and her eyes turned black like the black eyes of the animals that lived in the forest. When she was done, she put one of the beast's fearsome teeth on a bit of thread and hung it around her neck. She packed up her loom and her knitting needles, and she put on the cloak she had knit, and she set off into the forest to make her own way.

THE HARE AND THE STAG AND THE PRINCESS

nce upon a time, there was a beautiful castle. It sat atop a hill made of flowers, and its walls were made of diamonds.

In the tower of the castle lived a girl. She was kept there by the evil witch who owned the castle, who made the girl cook and clean and serve her. The witch had stolen her as a little girl, and she would never, ever let her go.

One day, while the witch was out hunting, a handsome woman came to the castle. The servant girl was in awe of her. Although she lived in a house made of diamonds, this woman was still the most beautiful thing she'd ever seen.

"You must be a princess," the servant girl said.

"I am a princess. But why must I be?"

"Because you have the face of an angel and the bearing of a queen. You must go far away from this place, for a wicked witch lives here, and she would love nothing more than to devour you," said the servant girl.

"You have blue eyes like the blue of the sky. Run away with me," said the princess. "We'll live happily, forever."

"I cannot go," the servant girl said. "I am only a servant, and you are a princess. I must stay here and serve the witch."

And so the princess went away sadly, and the servant girl wept into her mop bucket. When the witch returned, she brought a white hare in a sack. She threw the hare at the servant girl's feet.

"Servant girl, I have killed us a hare. You must clean it and dress it for dinner." Then the witch sat beside the fire and spun magic.

The girl reluctantly did as she was told, though she wept bitter tears to skin the poor creature. That night, the witch ate a glorious feast of hare and carrots, and when she had eaten her fill, she threw the servant girl the hare's leg bones.

"Eat up," the witch said as she laughed cruelly.

The girl took the hare's leg bones and used them to cure the soft white hide, and when the hide was cured, she wrapped the bones in it and kept it in her bed.

"You are my only friend," she told the skin of the hare. "When I am sad, I shall tell only you."

A few days later, the witch grew hungry again and announced that she would leave to go hunting. The girl made her a lunch and bid her farewell, but she whispered to the hare-skin that she hoped the witch would never return.

When the witch was gone, the princess returned. The servant girl was overjoyed to see her and threw her arms around her.

"You have dark hair like the dark of a shaded wood. Run away with me," said the princess, "and we'll live happily ever after."

"I cannot go," the servant girl replied, anguished. "I am only a servant, and you are a princess. I must stay here and serve the witch, and you must go, so you are not devoured."

And so the princess went away, and the girl wept into the earth as she weeded the garden. When the witch returned, she brought a white stag in a wheelbarrow. She dropped the carcass of the beautiful beast at the servant girl's feet.

"Servant girl, I have killed us a stag. Clean it and dress it for dinner," the witch ordered her and then went to sit by the fire and spin magic on her wheel.

The girl hated to see the beautiful creature dead, but she dared not disobey the witch. She wept bitter tears as she prepared the meal. That night, the witch ate a feast of venison and potatoes, and when she had eaten her fill, she threw the antlers to the servant girl and told her to eat.

The girl took the antlers and used them to cure the stag's beautiful white hide, and when the hide was cured, she wrapped the antlers in the hide and put them behind her door.

"You are my only protector," she told the stag-skin. "When I am afraid, I shall tell only you."

A few days after that, the witch grew hungry again and announced that she would leave to go hunting. The servant girl made her a lunch and bid her farewell, but after the witch was gone, the servant girl told the stag-hide that she hoped the witch never returned. She waited for the princess to visit her, but she never came. The servant girl wept into the feather-duster that she used to pull cobwebs out of the castle.

When the witch returned, she brought a strange shape in her wheelbarrow.

"Servant girl, I have killed us a princess. Clean it and dress it for dinner."

The girl's heart shattered into a million pieces when she saw that the wheelbarrow held the body of her very own princess, and she shook with sadness.

"I cannot do what you have asked me," she said to the witch.

The witch opened her mouth and shrieked with a sound like a thousand crows, and black smoke came out from her inhuman mouth and wrapped around the servant girl, suffocating her.

"Stop!" the girl begged. "Please, stop. I will do as you say."

The smoke released her, and the witch went to sit by the fire and spin magic.

The girl sobbed so much that she cried out the blue of her eyes, and they turned white—white as the fur of the hare—as she skinned the princess and prepared the witch's dinner. That night the witch ate a feast of princess and King's cress, and when she had eaten her fill, she threw the skull to the servant girl and told her to eat.

The girl took the skull to her room and put it beside her pillow, and she said, "You are my only love. When I am lonely, I shall tell only you."

A few days after that, the witch grew hungry again, and she went out hunting. The girl shook with terror at what the witch would kill this time. She cried to the hare-skin to comfort her. She begged the stag-skin to protect her. She pleaded with the princess's skull to forgive her. But her three friends sat there, silent, and their bones did nothing to help her. The girl stopped crying. She cleaned the cellar, and her eyes were dry.

When the witch returned, she was carrying a tiny bundle. She handed it to the servant girl.

"Servant girl, I have brought us a baby. Babies are best and most tender when they are fresh, you know. Leave it alive until you cook it, and then we will have dinner."

The girl's heart could not break because it had already shattered and blown away, but the sight of the helpless baby turned her mind to stone. All the color blanched from her rich dark hair, and her hair turned as white as the stag's hide.

"I will do as you say," the servant girl said.

The girl took the baby and waited until the witch sat down beside the fire to spin magic. As soon as the witch's chair creaked, the girl ran. She ran to the door of the castle made of diamonds, and she tried and tried to open it, but the door was woven shut with magic and would not move.

"I am so sorry, child. I want to save you, but the door is stuck fast and will not open," the girl said, and though her tears were all gone, the blue came back into her eyes. In an instant, the shimmering form of a hare appeared. He bowed to the girl, then used his powerful hind legs to kick down the door. The door opened.

"Thank you, my only friend," the girl said, and she ran outside.

Once outside, she ran as fast as she could down the path, but soon the path disappeared. The hill made of flowers had swallowed it, as it swallowed everything, and it was beginning to swallow up the girl's legs. She fought and struggled and screamed, but the flowers were spun of magic, and no matter how she tried she only sunk deeper.

"I am so sorry, child. I want to save you, but my legs are stuck fast and I cannot move," the girl said, and though her mind had turned to stone, the brown came back into her hair. A moment later, the shimmering form of a stag appeared. He bowed to the girl, then used his mighty antlers to scoop great loads of flowers away, tossing them into the breeze. The ground appeared, solid and unenchanted, beneath her feet.

"Thank you, my only protector," the servant girl said, and she ran down the hill.

At the bottom of the hill was a village. The village was full of people screaming, and sobbing, and running to and fro. The girl was afraid, and she hid the sleeping baby on her back.

"Excuse me," she called to a young boy. "Why is everyone screaming and crying?"

"A terrible witch has stolen a baby from its cradle," the boy said. "The villagers are despairing, for no one is brave enough to go and face her."

The girl asked the boy to take her to the child's parents. When they saw their baby safe and sound on the girl's back, they collapsed in joyful tears and kissed the girl's cheeks.

"You must stay with us," the mother said. "I will make a feast."

"I cannot stay," the girl said. "I am not a hero. I am only a servant, and I must do what is right."

The girl spent all night wandering the forests at the foot of the hill made of flowers, thinking of how to defeat the witch. She heard the villagers singing and dancing happily in the village, and she knew they must be protected. She walked alone, her heart and mind sad, and scared, and lonely.

"I'm so sorry, village. I want to save you, but the witch is strong and I am weak."

A moment later, the shimmering form of the princess appeared. She took the girl in her arms and pressed a kiss to her lips.

"I miss you," the girl whispered. "I should have run away with you when you first asked. But I didn't. And now I can't run away. I have to see this through. But I don't know how."

"I miss you, too," the princess said. "But we will be together soon. You are stronger than you know." And she bent, and plucked a flower, and gave it to her.

In that moment, the girl knew exactly what to do. Before morning, she picked many handfuls of yellow flowers, stuffing them into her pockets and into her dress. As the sun rose, she started back up the hill made of flowers, and the ground appeared beneath her feet with every step. The rising sun shone off the diamond walls of the castle with a blinding beauty. The girl walked straight into the castle, the door opening before her.

She marched through the castle until she stood before the witch at the fire.

"I have brought you a servant girl," the servant girl said. "Clean me and dress me for dinner."

The witch rose up with a shriek of rage at the sight of the girl, and in a second, she had killed her.

That night, the witch ate a magnificent banquet of servant girl and yellow ladyslipper flowers, and when she was done, she looked at the skull of the servant girl and laughed.

A moment later, the shimmering form of a hare appeared in front of her and the shining form of a stag and the ghostly form of the princess and then the bright spirit of the servant girl, holding a flower.

"Eat up." The servant girl smiled and tossed the flower to the witch.

The witch looked at herself and realized that she, too, was a shadowy form. She looked down at her own body on the floor, holding the ghost of a poison flower. The witch opened her mouth and shrieked with the sound of a thousand birds, and her ghostly form shattered into feathers. The girl and the princess smiled and joined hands and walked into the forest with the hare and the stag. And there, they did not live, but were happy ever after.

OLD MERRY MOONEY

*I*n a village, in a country, in a land far away, old Merry Mooney lived in a simple cottage. Her cottage was at the edge of town, at the far end of the street, where the dust and dirt began to gobble up the cobblestone. She lived alone, and she talked to people no one else could see, and the townsfolk thought she might be a witch. She did have a cat, after all. Two cats, in fact, and no husband, so what else could she be but a witch? A witch who spent her days on her porch, carving wooden dolls, and talking to nobody.

Merry didn't mind what the villagers whispered. She had always liked cats, and solitude, and she had never liked husbands. They appeared a generally unpleasant phenomena, like typhoons, or toothaches. No, she much preferred to sit alone and carve her dolls and talk to the faerie folk.

The faerie folk lived in the shrubbery and bushes that dotted the hillsides, in the underbrush, near the mushroom rings, in the burbling little canyons of streams. They crept along the edges of the village, looking for offerings of bread and milk. In the old days, every family had left out bread and milk for the faerie folk, hoping to curry favor or avoid wrath. As time went on, they had stopped believing, and now old Merry Mooney was the only one left who paid any attention to the old ways.

Fickle, the faeries always had been. Forgetful, they never were. So the old woman had a steady stream of pixies, wee men, brownies, and the like, coming to her doorstep. She fed them and chatted with them and spent long dark nights watching the moon with them, but she never let them come in, and she never accepted their gifts.

One day, a faerie with eyes like a winter's day came to the cottage. They were so thin, they were transparent, and their voice was a December wind. Merry Mooney heard them crying outside her window and came out onto her porch, carrying a bowl of milk and bread.

"Hungry?" she asked, offering the bowl.

"I cannot eat," wailed the cold little faerie. "My body is melting away, and surely I will die."

Merry thought hard about what to say. To offer help to the fae could be dangerous; to spurn them could be fatal.

The little shadow shivered pitifully.

"Well, make your request, then," Merry said. "And I'll think it over."

"Make me a new body," the faerie begged. "One that will not melt away."

Merry Mooney laughed. "Ask your own kind, faerie. I have no magic. I cannot make you a body."

"Do not laugh at me, Merry Mooney," the faerie warned. Merry's heart froze at the sound of her name. "Yes, woman, I have your name. If you do not make me a body, I will take you back to faerie land to be my servant. But if you make me a body that cannot melt and cannot freeze and that suits me, I will be your faithful companion, and I will protect you all your days."

Merry Mooney knew she had no choice. The faerie had her name, and she was at their whim.

"As you wish," Merry said. "I will make you a body."

So Merry sat down at her table and made a little doll out of cloth while her cats purred at her feet. The doll had a pretty skirt and embroidery floss hair and a face made of needlework.

The next day, the faerie returned. They were colder than ever.

"Well, well, Merry Mooney, and where is my body?"

Merry presented the faerie with the little cloth doll. "Here is a body I have made you that will never melt and never freeze," she said.

"This will not do," the faerie said. "This body has long hair and skirts like a washer woman, and I am not like a washer woman. Try again."

So that night, Merry Mooney sat at her table and made a little doll out of paper, while her cats snoozed in their basket. The doll had a smart hat and a handsome jacket and a face made of charcoal scratchings.

The next day, the faerie returned. They were thinner than ever.

"Well, well, Merry Mooney, and where is my body?"

Merry brought the little paper doll to the faerie. "Here is a body that will never melt and never freeze and has no hair and no skirts."

"This will not do," the faerie said. "This body has a hat and a jacket like a village boy, and I am not like a village boy. Try again."

That night, Merry Mooney sat at her kitchen table and wept,

while the cats batted a ball of string back and forth. She did not know what else to do. She did not know how to make a body for the faerie, and she did not want to be a servant in faerie land. When the sun rose on the horizon, Merry Mooney got up and went to the yard. She found a sturdy branch and began to carve.

In the afternoon, the faerie returned. They were fading away, barely a chilly breeze.

"Well, well, Merry Mooney," the faerie whispered. "Are you ready to go to faerie land and be my servant?"

Merry presented the wooden doll she had carved. "Here is the body I have made you. It will never melt and never freeze, it has no hair and no skirts, it has no hat and no jacket, and it is entirely your own."

The faerie was delighted and slipped into the wooden doll like you or I would slip into a coat. They held out their wooden arms and stretched their wooden feet and made faces with their carved wooden face.

"You have fulfilled our bargain, Merry Mooney," the faerie said, and bowed. "I will be your faithful companion, and protect you all your days."

Soon, word of what Merry had done began to spread through faerie land, and other faeries began to seek her help, for faeries cannot stay forever in the human lands in their own bodies. A nymph asked for a body of porcelain and suede; a pixie asked for a body of cloth. And Merry Mooney helped the faeries, in exchange for their promises of protection. This went on and on for many years, until Merry lost track of time. One after the other, her cats grew old and died, and Merry was all alone.

The villagers began to grow uneasy. There were whispered rumors that the dolls that Merry Mooney made had an uncanny liveliness and had even been seen wandering the cobblestone streets at night. Things began to go missing from the villagers' houses, food and trinkets disturbed in the night. One day, Farmer Greene's dairy cow was found dead in the field, eaten down to the bones by tiny, porcelain teeth.

"It's the witch," the townsfolk began to murmur. "She's been summoning devils to curse us all!"

Merry tried to keep the peace. She told the faeries that they must stop tormenting the village folk.

"Ah, but we only swore to protect you, Merry Mooney," the wooden faerie that she had first helped told her. "Our bargain is upheld, and you cannot stop us from doing what we may."

Then one night, one of the Smith's children disappeared. She showed up three days later in a flowered field with black eyes and an eerie smile and the people whispered she was a changeling. The priest tried to pray over her, and the Smiths cried over her, and the whole town implored her to return to herself. She only blinked those black eyes, and smiled that eerie smile, and sang songs she'd never known before.

"It's the witch's fault!" the people cried. "The witch must be killed!"

They lit torches and marched down the street, determined to burn Merry Mooney in her house. As soon as their feet crossed the line of her garden, however, an army of faeries materialized before them.

"Go home," Merry Mooney warned the townsfolk. "You cannot harm me."

Enraged and blinded by their ignorance, the townsfolk roared forward, tools and weapons raised to kill Merry and raze her home. The faeries fell upon them, with long teeth and sharp claws, with poison bites and stinging vines, until every man in the village had been chewed down to the bone. And Merry Mooney stood on her porch and wept to see it happen.

"We will keep our oath to you, Merry," said the wooden faerie, and blood dripped down their beautiful wooden face. "We will protect you always as we have for the last hundred years."

Merry was filled with horror as she realized how many years had gone by without her notice. She knew, then, that the faeries had enslaved her after all and that they would never let her go. They had made her something more—or less than—human without taking her to faerie land at all.

That evening, the women and children of the village all stood around Merry Mooney's house and wailed as the blood of their husbands and fathers soaked into Merry's flowerbeds. They cried and cried a salt circle around Merry's house, and Merry went into her shed and fetched a shovel.

For the next few days, Merry dug and dug. She dug graves for the men who had died coming to kill her. She dug them all around her home—circle of shallow graves for the men who had been foolish enough to call her a witch. When the digging was done, Merry washed her hands, bringing a bowl of bread and milk to her porch and a keg of dandelion wine and summoned the faeries to her.

"Thank you for your help, my friends," she said. "To celebrate our victory, we will drink and dance beneath the moonlight."

The faeries took the wine and made music in the night. Tiny porcelain hands wrapped around cloth waists, embroidered teeth gleamed in the starlight, and wooden feet beat the earth like a drum. They drank and sang and filled the empty village with the noises of an uncanny celebration. By dawn, they had all fallen into a drunken stupor and were sleeping on Merry Mooney's lawn.

And Merry Mooney, who had never been a witch before, stayed up all night doing her first spell. A growing spell, a speeding spell. She chanted her spell over the graves of the village men, again and again, and toadstools sprung from their corpses. As the first rays of dawn reached over the hills, the final mushroom sprouted into place, and the circle was complete. The village wavered and flickered before Merry's eyes before disappearing entirely.

When the faeries began to awaken, they found themselves returned to their original faerie forms—for the fashioned bodies Merry made for them could not make the trip into faerie land. Yes, Merry, the newly minted witch, had grown a faerie circle overnight, and taken them all away from the village. The faeries began to screech and scream, but when they went to rip Merry's flesh from her bones, they could not. Their bargain still bound them, even here, and they found they were not able to harm the old woman in any way.

Merry sat on her porch and hummed to herself as the faeries shrieked behind her. The faerie sun felt brighter, better, than the old village sun ever had. And the old woman was content.

As for the village, the next morning the widows and children awoke to find the witch's cottage entirely gone. All that remained was a circle of graves and a field scattered with hundreds of splayed and empty dolls. No one dared enter the circle, so they tossed burning torches into it and set the grass ablaze.

The village went on, and in time, everyone forgot. No one was left to put out milk or bread, and no faerie stepped foot there again. The Smiths' changeling daughter grew up and married a baker and lived an exemplary imitation of a human life—although she did sometimes sneak out of the house to dance naked in the moonlight.

Time erased most of Merry Mooney from the village, but the children there still prefer teddy bears and balls and jacks. They have a wariness of dolls, especially those with a certain emptiness behind the eyes. For they just might be one of Merry Mooney's creations, waiting to give a faerie a home.

Journey of the Rusalkas

Jaclyn Wilmoth

As the seizures rock me, lies fall from my skin, sprinkling on the ground like confetti at a party gone overboard. It is the Sacred Disease, say the Greeks, full of demons and gods and premonitions, all fighting inside until my memories run away, and I am left lifted. I mistake myself for Selene, Eve, Artemis, Lilith, as they set fire to my brain. And the only memory that is left is falling, falling, and a splash.

ask me the future
mad passion exposed at once
floating and sinking

This is how it is when you forget the memories you hold, when you have only future and no past. I am no longer drowned by my lover for the child inside. Some secrets are too great, even for weddings. No, instead: the moon falls so in love with me that it slips inside me, shakes me into the river, going down with me, making the night a watery dark until the world is so black that all the stars fall. I wait in the waters. Wait until our child is no more than a will-o-wisp. Wait until my red hair turns green, growing longer than me and swaying as fish nibble it. Wait for those who come near the water at night, so that my seaweed hair can grasp them, tickle them as they gulp the water, convulsing and rocking, floating, sinking with me.

wrinkled skin and locks
wet that hold me trapped away
unquiet rocking

But it isn't all bad. In June, when the air gets warm and summer comes, I lift myself from the river, hair never dry, and walk amongst the fields. My breasts, my head, drips with the water I've drank in all year and the crops drink of me. The fluorescent green weeds, vines, grass, trees, food are thirsty for my muck.

at night in willow
and birch I swing as water
flies seedlings suckle

And I wonder if all this would be moot if my head had never closed up. Maybe like cave paintings, I should drill a hole in my crown, let the gods out, let the demons that fill my brain free, and let the air and water in. Press my fingernails into my skull and open it. So that there's balance between what's inside my head and what's outside. So that the lies dissolve in the nighttime sky, so that the memories come back. So that the heavy, airy, too-full density of my brain isn't shaking, floating, sinking.

so the moon goes out
split in two, breathe through the brain
so the stars come in

The Curse of Agatha Franke

What ghosts are you willing to live with?

Elle Campbell

))🌙🌑🌕🌑((

gatha Franke never meant to be a witch. It happened, as they say, quite by accident.

Yes, Agatha slipped into her witchiness one subtle, oblivious step at a time. It started with the rocks and twigs and snippets of plants she collected as she walked barefoot in the woods, just outside the Karlsville town limits. A loose piece of granite bouncing in her apron pocket to boost her energy. A slender willow bough that had fallen during a summer thunderstorm, perfect for clearing a head when thoughts became muddled. A sprig of rosemary resting on her kitchen windowsill, an invitation for good memories to visit and stay a spell.

When those simple charms and snippets of folk wisdom worked, helping Agatha smooth out the rougher edges of life, she grew more confident. Magic, Agatha knew, was mostly the right combination of plants, common sense, and strong will. But with time, she gradually took on more complicated spells, intuitive weavings of herbs, lunar timing, and incantations. She didn't take this magic lightly, at least not at first, and she used it selflessly. Her life was a quiet one, lived alone in her tiny, two-bedroom cottage just off Main Street, and as such, it was easy to cultivate the calm and serenity she craved. Her more complex magic was reserved for the people of Karlsville. Sleeping charms for exhausted mothers. Protection spells when the young men left town seeking adventure and fortune. A well-timed hex if word got 'round that a husband wasn't treating his wife with the proper respect.

(Nothing wrong with that, thought Agatha, as long as the person deserved it.)

Agatha Franke was a witch all right, but for a long time, everyone failed to recognize it, viewing her, instead, as a helpful (albeit uncomfortably straightforward) aunt. Then the incident at Town Hall happened.

Mayor Karl—yes, like *Karl*sville—went on a half-cracked tangent about how front-yard gardens were "ruining the integrity of the neighborhoods." Agatha, whose own front yard was a lovingly tended tangle of vegetables, flowers, and herbs, jumped out of her seat, pointed a long finger at the mayor, and said what every soul in that room was thinking.

"If you want to restore integrity to our neighborhoods, *Ernest*," she spat his first name, "you might want to start by being a little more discreet with your girlfriend's visits every time your wife is out of town. Leave my gardens the hell alone."

A chorus of gasps filled the room. They may have all been thinking it, but no one had actually thought to say it. Then Ernest Karl, sweating and purple-faced, banged his wooden gavel and yelled, "Agatha Franke, you goddamn witch, mind your own business!"

Mayor Karl's shouted words acted as a spell of their own, and suddenly, the whole town, including Agatha, could see exactly what she was. Then, just as quickly, they all decided that if Agatha, with her herbal remedies and healing touch and plain-worded wisdom, was a witch, they didn't quite mind having one around. In fact, it seemed like the type of character any self-respecting town should have.

Agatha bore no shame about her new label. Indeed, she embraced it. A couple of weeks later, a small family of geese with sleek, chestnut-colored bodies and midnight beaks and feet nested in her yard. When they stayed on through the bitter cold of winter, Agatha figured that made them hers, and she coddled them like a mother spoils her babes. They didn't have the same glamor as Circe's lions, but Agatha wasn't a glamorous person, and she appreciated how honest and ornery they were. They'd waddle through town, tail feathers shaking as they hissed and spat at pedestrians, and Agatha would trail behind, nodding regally at her exasperated neighbors. It was a testament to how beloved and feared Agatha was that an unkind word was never uttered, publicly or privately, about her cranky, ill-mannered pets.

One cold, autumn night, not long after midnight, Agatha was awakened by a sharp *rap-rap-rap*. This didn't surprise her. Most of the folks around town were private people, and if they needed help, they typically didn't want everyone jawing about it, which was wont to happen in small towns. Agatha wrapped her favorite shawl around her shoulders and padded barefoot to her back door, where a small form shivered on her stoop.

"Ah, Beatrice." Agatha gathered the girl—well, Agatha supposed she was a woman now—into her arms and helped her into the cottage. Beatrice's shoulders, slight and bent, shook with sobs as Agatha got her situated at the small kitchen table then went to put the kettle on.

Beatrice's mother, Katherine, had been a childhood friend of Agatha's, and the witch had watched Bea grow from infancy. She'd always been a bright little thing with shining eyes and golden curls, and when she was younger, she'd spent many hours helping Agatha in her garden. In recent years, Bea's attention had shifted from flowers and herbs to the young gentlemen of Karlsville, and Agatha had been happy to hear about her engagement. While Agatha enjoyed her solitary life, she could always tell that Bea was meant for a partnership, children. . . a family of her own.

But the gossip mill had been spinning furiously earlier that day. Bea's fiancé, a longtime beau before he went away to university, had sent word that he was breaking off the engagement.

"I can't do it, Ag." Bea slumped onto the table with a groan, her blue eyes almost swollen shut from crying. Misery poured off the girl, so dark and tumultuous that Agatha could see her potted herbs shrink and wilt with sympathy.

"You don't have a choice." Agatha wasn't unkind, but she always spoke plainly.

"But you do." Bea looked up at her with hope, her wet cheeks glistening in the moonlight. "You know so much. I know there's something you could do. Something. I can't feel like this, Agatha. I can't face—I can't face all of them. . ." She swung an arm out, gesturing toward town. "I'm so ashamed. I can't do it. I can't."

"A broken heart's nothing to be ashamed of." Agatha poured water for tea as she talked, adding a pinch of lavender to Bea's. "There's no fault in falling in love."

Bea's eyes narrowed. "Is that what you tell poor Will Lind?"

Agatha's cheeks burned hot. Will Lind had spent the better part of twenty years in love with Agatha, and the whole town knew it. But she had seen too much of marriage to want any part in it herself. The fact that even the geese seemed to like Will, preening flirtatiously whenever he stopped by, was not lost on Agatha, but she preferred not to think about it.

"Never you mind Will Lind." She gestured at Bea's tea. "Drink up, and I'll work up an herbal bath for you."

By the time Bea finished her tea, Agatha had filled a drawstring bag with salts and herbs—rose, lavender, and lemon balm to calm the nerves. The girl's throat bobbed with resignation—clearly she'd been hoping for something more—but she whispered a polite "Thank you, ma'am" and took her leave, the crisp leaves crunching beneath her boots as she walked toward home.

Agatha, tired and ready to return to bed, collected the empty mugs and carried them to the sink. As she did so, she tilted Bea's and glanced curiously at the dregs. The tea leaves, lumpy and damp, formed two intersecting lines. A clear, distinct X. Now, Agatha wasn't a nervous woman, but she didn't at all like that X, which was usually a warning of trouble to come. That night, as she tried to fall back to sleep, she tossed and turned, double guessing her assumption that Bea's heartache was the run-of-the-mill kind, the type that would heal with time and courage.

In the weeks that followed, Agatha kept a close eye on Bea whenever she went to town. She expected red eyes and a subdued demeanor, especially at first, but to her dismay, Bea began to withdraw altogether. She showed up for her job at the general store, but she appeared to shrink into herself, her smiles flat and her cheeks sunken and pale. The sparkle and shine that had made her one of the most sought-after girls in town had been snuffed out. When Agatha, her voice lowered to a discreet whisper, asked Bea if the baths had helped, Bea answered with a noncommittal shrug, never quite meeting Agatha's gaze. All the way home, the geese, picking up on Agatha's mood, plagued passersby with angry honks and reached toward skirts and jacket sleeves with snapping beaks.

By early winter, when Agatha's flower beds were barren and the topsoil was frozen solid from the long, cold nights, it seemed like Bea had disappeared altogether. Her dresses hung limp and loose. Her movements were slow and labored as she fetched items at the store for customers. Her voice, which she rarely used anymore, was a dry, raspy whisper. Bea's mother dropped in on Agatha for a visit one blustery morning, and over coffee and scones, she confessed that every single morning, before she got out of bed, she prayed with all her might that Bea would still be alive.

"It's not as bad as that." Agatha was taken aback. "Is it?"

Her gaggle of geese was curled up by the fireplace, wrapped around each other in a tangle of floppy feet and feathers. It was a cozy sight, domestic and soothing, but Agatha's mind was dragged back to that dark, foreboding X at the bottom of Bea's teacup.

"Maybe I'm being dramatic, but I'm scared, Agatha." Katherine picked at her mulberry scone with her fork, and Agatha realized her guest had been too upset to eat, even though the flaky scones had always been her favorite. "At first, I thought she'd bounce back, but she just keeps sinking deeper. It's not like . . . *that* has never happened before. Remember that girl who got jilted in Irma?"

Agatha remembered. The girl was missing for days before her poor family found her body in the woods, swinging from the tree where she and her boy had carved their initials. Just thinking about it made her throat burn with bile.

A few days later, Agatha was ready for the *rap-rap-rap* on her door in the dead of night. She'd known it was coming. She'd spent the time since Katherine's visit pondering this new information about the depth of Beatrice's melancholy. Most of the time, Agatha's magic felt like a gift, a way to help and assist her friends and neighbors. The power she wielded came easily to her, and she suffered no crisis of conscience over aiding overwhelmed wives or protecting the farmers' crops. But she knew what Bea would ask of her, the weight of the magic required, and this time, the decisions Agatha had to make felt like a burden.

Agatha opened the door, and a gust of snow and frigid wind blew inside. The geese, at their customary spot in front of the warm fireplace, hissed in displeasure.

"Come in," Agatha said.

The wraith who entered Agatha's cottage bore no resemblance to the old Beatrice, a girl who had bubbled with laughter and trilled bawdy songs as she helped Agatha transplant seedlings each spring. Tonight, Bea wore a dark, velvet cloak, and beneath her hood, her once round cheeks jutted severely and her hair hung greasy and uncombed. She may not have physically harmed herself yet, but Agatha could tell with one glance that, in her heart, Bea already had one foot in the grave.

All over a boy. Agatha almost clicked her tongue with distaste.

This time, Agatha already had tea prepared, but when she put a mug before Bea at the kitchen table, the girl made no move to touch it. She stared up at Agatha with hollow eyes.

"I don't want to feel anymore."

Agatha took a deep breath. She'd been prepared for this, had planned a whole speech for Bea about why this magic, in particular, was no good. Yes, there was a spell Agatha knew, but it was too dark, the price too high.

"You don't want to do this, Bea," Agatha began. She reached out, tried to cover the girl's hand with her own, but Bea pulled back.

"I don't want to feel anything anymore." Bea hardly moved her lips as she forced the words out. "It hurts. I'm done."

Agatha opened her mouth to refuse. It wasn't like she'd never told someone no before. Grieving families who became so obsessed with contacting the dead that they stopped living. Discarded husbands who wanted their wives back, when Agatha knew very well they'd treated them worse than cattle. Hexes aimed at victims over petty misunderstandings. Agatha refused to perform magic all the time.

But in that moment, all Agatha could remember was the X at the bottom of Bea's teacup. The story about the girl from Irma. The look of worry on Katherine's face. Bea was one bad decision away from tragedy, and the stony way she'd uttered those words, "I'm done," nagged at Agatha. What exactly was Bea done with? Love? Men? Living?

"Listen close to me, Beatrice Eklund." Agatha sank onto a hard, wooden chair, so she was eye to eye with this shell of a girl. "If that's what you really want, to no longer feel, it's not something that can be undone. It's permanent, unable—"

"Good." Bea's voice was flat.

"The spell is difficult. Harrowing, even. It might even be pain—"

"I don't care."

With a sigh, Agatha walked Bea through the spell step by step. Candlelight flickered around them, throwing the deep grooves of Bea's cheeks into sharp relief, and Agatha watched her carefully for even a flicker of fear or disgust. But Bea never wavered, holding the witch's gaze steadily throughout.

"And we can do it tonight?" she asked.

Agatha nodded, her mouth set in a grim line. Through whatever twist of fate, Bea had picked the full moon to visit. Any other day, and Agatha would have had to put her off, but full moons were ideal for release, for letting go, for loosening your grip on outdated ideas.

Tonight was the perfect time to freeze a heart.

Usually, Agatha reserved the icebox for bad-tempered

husbands. It was simple to pay a visit to their wives and collect some stray whiskers or a crescent of fingernail from the floor. At the next full moon, they'd go into the icebox, along with the right herbs and the right words, and then, as if by magic, Agatha would stop hearing stories about how so-and-so had to hide her bruises. Agatha liked the icebox. It was simple, elegant, effective. But she'd never used it like this before.

Working in tandem, the two women gathered the necessary supplies, digging through Agatha's jars and tiny clay pots to collect rue, chamomile, and witch hazel. Bea, who'd been so like a ghost when she'd arrived, worked with feverish focus now, doing as Agatha instructed and imbuing every moment, every touch with intention. When they were almost ready, Agatha roused the sleeping geese from the fire—all but one—and shepherded them outside to their lean-to next to the cottage. Agatha's chest gave a vicious twist when she eyed her precious gaggle, wondering if the remaining geese would ever forgive her for the betrayal she was about to commit.

When Agatha got back in the cottage, Bea had done as she'd requested and stripped down to her shift. The thin, white cotton did nothing to protect her against the chill of the winter night, and even in the firelight, Agatha could see the goosebumps raised along her emaciated arms and calves. On her lap, Bea had gathered the remaining goose, a quiet, sweet-tempered hen named Mabel, and the two curved into each other, sharing warmth. When Agatha drew close, she could hear Bea murmuring to the goose as her fingers ran over its sleek feathers, "Good goose. So beautiful. So brave."

The spell had already begun.

"You're sure about this?" Agatha asked, one final time. "You understand the price?"

Bea's gaze never left the dark, beady eyes of the goose in her arms. "Pretty, pretty girl," she crooned, her voice soothing. But to Agatha, she gave a swift, decisive nod.

Agatha threw some dried herbs on the fire, watched them spark and sizzle, then she walked 'round and 'round, circling Bea and the goose with bright red string. The color of blood, life force, the heart. She left the string loose at first, until she was sure the goose's wings would be contained, then, with a sinking heart and a deft flick of her wrist, she pulled it tight, binding girl and goose together. She waited for the goose to panic, to lash out, but it turned to her with still, calm eyes. As if it already knew, and accepted, its fate.

"Now repeat after me," Agatha instructed, and Bea nodded

solemnly, keeping her eyes locked on the bird cradled in her arms.

"Heart to heart, and chest to chest,
Eye to eye, and breath to breath,
You are me, and I am thee,
What happens to you, be done to me."

Agatha repeated it twice more, Bea carefully following her words, then hissed, "Keep going." Bea's measured murmurs filled the cottage until each sound ran and slid together, no longer sounding like words at all. A breeze rushed over them, lifting Bea's hair and ruffling the goose's feathers, as if a window or door had flown open, but instead of the frigid cold of the night air, this draft was warm. Hot even.

The spell was working. And even though Agatha had a hundred reservations, a thousand regrets, part of her delighted in the rush of it. The thrill. This was real power, this energy coursing down her arms and into her fingertips. For months, everyone in town had sat idle, watching Beatrice get more and more lost in her own grief, but Agatha...Agatha was doing something about it. Agatha didn't have to watch her sweet little garden helper waste away from a broken heart. Agatha didn't have to sit on her hands and just hope that Bea got better someday. Agatha was going to make her better.

"Now," Agatha whispered.

When Agatha had bound Bea and the goose, she'd been careful to leave one of Bea's hands free. Bea, still muttering the incantation, didn't hesitate. In her fingers, she gripped a small knife, its silver blade glinting in the light of the flames, and in one swift motion, she plunged it into the goose's soft, downy breast.

But it was Bea who screamed.

When it was all over, Agatha and Bea tidied the cottage. Bea's shift, stained beyond repair, was burned, and Agatha disposed of Mabel's blood in the nearby creek, so the taint of sacrifice would wash away with the clear, rushing water. And in the icebox sat a small heart, a deep, maroon red. Frozen.

"Thank you." Bea stood on Agatha's porch, shoulders back, eyes clear. In an hour, day would break, and she had to get home. Her lips lifted, a semblance of a smile, and it didn't have the warmth it once did, but neither did it carry the tortured anguish of just a few hours earlier. Agatha's own heart was heavy, her stomach leaden with grief over the loss of her beloved pet, but she couldn't regret helping Bea. With a wave, she sent the girl home.

* * *

Over the upcoming days, Agatha kept close tabs on Beatrice. The girl started putting on weight, gaining back some of her comely figure. At work, she talked with the customers again, exchanging greetings and basic social niceties. If she appeared somehow flat to Agatha, not as buoyant and radiant as she had once been, it was still a vast improvement over the oppressive gloom that previously held her hostage. Indeed, the entire town heaved a sigh of relief at Bea's placid smiles and unshakeable composure.

The loss of Mabel still stung. The other geese didn't seem to blame or resent Agatha, but that only added to her guilt. How could she have betrayed a love so pure, so unconditional? But at the time, Agatha knew, it had felt like a choice between the goose and Beatrice, and she simply couldn't bring herself to resign the little girl she'd known, the one who'd woven daisy chains in her garden, to such a cruel fate.

By the time winter solstice approached, Agatha was feeling confident in her choice. Her biggest worry had been that Bea's frozen heart might make her cruel or unkind, but that day at the store, Agatha had witnessed one of the town's children drop the penny candy he'd just purchased, and it had broken to pieces on the floor. Before the child could begin to cry, Bea had replaced it, free of charge, a smile on her face that didn't quite reach her eyes. Agatha had given Bea the equanimity she'd asked for; she hadn't turned her into some Frankenstein's monster.

On the evening of solstice, the longest night of the year, Agatha put a special Yule log on the hearth and made mulled wine, breathing in the spicy aroma of cinnamon and cloves. She observed the holiday, as she did most things, on her own, but the little cottage felt festive, hung with pine boughs and lit with candles. The wine warmed her blood and filled her head with a pleasant hum, while outside, the stars shone a crisp, brilliant white in the inky sky. She had just changed into her nightgown and was getting ready to bank the fire when the whistling snores of the geese were interrupted by a soft noise, a faint *scratch-scratch-scratch*.

"For crying out loud," Agatha muttered, shuffling to the door. She'd been in a fine mood and was not inclined to ruin it dealing with someone's philandering husband or overwrought teenage daughter. She was ready to say as much, too. But when she swung the heavy wooden door open, she froze, and not because of the bitter wind that pulled at her thin nightgown.

On Agatha's porch, wearing a short-sleeved dress and pinafore, stood a small girl. Her cheeks were dimpled, her eyes unnaturally bright. Even standing in the warmth of the cottage, Agatha's body was tensed against the cold, but this slip of a girl with her bare arms and legs seemed unaffected. She stared up at Agatha, expectant, but the witch couldn't quite catch her breath.

"B—Beatrice?" Agatha croaked. But not Beatrice now. Not the young woman who worked at the store and was old enough to be a bride. This was the Beatrice of a decade ago or more, short and spindly, no more than six or seven. Agatha felt another burst of cold, but it was not from the wind. It was like the fabric of time had been rent, with years long past rewoven into places they didn't belong. It was not natural.

The little girl laughed. The sound was merry enough, but Agatha still wanted to slam and lock the door.

"No, silly goose." The girl laughed again, and Agatha had to suppress a shudder. "I'm Kate. Beatrice is my mommy."

"Beatrice has no daughter." She was only eighteen now, on the cusp of nineteen. A daughter this age was impossible. And yet, as Agatha observed her, she could see that the little girl was exactly what Beatrice's daughter would look like. She was a perfect replica of Bea at that age, with a heart-shaped face and round blue eyes. But now Agatha could see that the girl's hair, twisted into neat plaits, was a warm, sandy brown, darker than Bea's. The contribution of an unknown, phantom father.

Kate pouted, her tiny lip pushing forward sullenly and her fists propped on her narrow hips. "She was going to. Until you ruined it."

Agatha was shaking now, her terror creeping beneath the surface of her skin. Swiftly, she stepped back and moved to shut the door—to shut out this unnerving little creature, whatever it was—but the girl's hand shot out and wrapped around Agatha's wrist, holding her in a grip too tight for a small child.

"You don't want to do that," the child warned, all former traces of joy or silliness gone. Her fingers were hot and feverish on Agatha's skin, almost burning, and again Agatha noticed that despite her short sleeves and knee-length skirt, the child seemed unphased by the winter cold. Agatha jerked against her grasp, hard, but the girl clung tighter.

"Invite me in, Agatha."

"Are—are you a ghost then?"

Agatha had dealt with ghosts a time or two, spirits stuck

between this world and the next. They had been cold souls, bound by fear, hatred, or trauma. Ultimately, they'd welcomed liberation from their earthly ties. Agatha had never, however, experienced a supernatural being like this, so corporeal. And the girl's heat . . . like all the warmth a body would produce in a lifetime, condensed into this present moment. Her vitality clarified into this tiny point of unlived potential.

The child shrugged. "Maybe." She paused to consider. "Most ghosts are an after. Life after life. I am a before. Life before life."

Panic made Agatha strong. With a wrench, she twisted her arm free and jumped back, slamming the door with a bang that had the geese grumbling and fluttering in their sleep. Sliding the deadbolt into place, she slumped against the door, heart pummeling against her breastbone.

"Fool," she whispered to herself. She'd overstepped. She could see that now. For all her magic, for all the charms and spells and rituals she'd performed over the years, for herself and others, none of them had filled her with the strange dread she'd felt while freezing Beatrice's heart. Or the same electrifying power. In the days since, she'd convinced herself that it was the same, no different from any other magic she performed, but she knew better. If it had been the same, she wouldn't have tried so hard to talk Bea out of it. And now there was a spirit outside her door, the remnant of an alternative course of events. The events that were meant to have happened.

Cursing under her breath, Agatha rushed to the window. The wind blew harder now, kicking up snowflakes into a swirl of impenetrable white, and Agatha squinted, trying to see if the little girl was still on her porch or if she'd moved on. She pulled her shawl tighter around her shoulders, but the cold was inside her, a block of ice deep in her chest that trickled out to her fingertips and toes.

"I told you not to do that."

Agatha froze at the sound of the girl's voice. She usually didn't have to look for courage, but it took every ounce of her considerable will to turn and look at the small figure who was sitting in her rocking chair, legs swinging over the edge. The chair, however, stayed eerily still. Kate grinned, dimples flashing as if she'd told a funny joke. There was no way the girl could have gotten inside the cottage. Agatha had closed the door too quickly.

"What do you want?" Agatha asked.

The girl shrugged. "I don't get to want. I don't get to play. I don't get to talk—to anyone but you, that is. Because you made me. I don't get to eat or make friends or get hugs. I just am."

Agatha squeezed herself against the door, torn between horror and sympathy. And guilt. The guilt yawned open inside her until she choked on it, a sandy lump in her throat. "What am I supposed to do?"

The girl shrugged again, and her face pulled into a spiteful grimace. "You know so much. Figure it out."

* * *

Bea's daughter-who-would-never-be was quiet at first. That first night, Agatha eventually curled up on the couch, and they'd eyed each other in a silent showdown until the sun crept over the horizon. Agatha thought the girl might disappear at that point, burned away like morning fog by the day's bright rays, but the little figure remained, perched on Agatha's favorite chair. Agatha's eyes drifted closed then, her exhaustion finally outweighing her horror, and when she woke a couple of hours later, groggy and stiff limbed, the girl was still there. Staring.

Unsure what else to do, Agatha moved through her daily routine. Feeding the geese. Collecting eggs from the chickens. Sweeping the wood floors and making her bed. Kate followed her through it all, a tiny shadow that made no noise and disrupted nothing. Agatha saw her reach out to touch a hen, a glittering mound of snow, a book of fairytales, but whatever object she tried to touch never budged, her fingers moving right through it as if she didn't even exist.

Because she didn't.

In the afternoon, Agatha walked into town, hopeful that she could escape the child for an hour or so. But Kate followed Agatha and her geese right out the door. The geese rustled nervously, feathers ruffling, but as far as Agatha could tell, they couldn't see the little girl skipping next to them, her skirts bouncing and bare arms swinging.

The general store was busy. Christmas was only a few days away, and the mood was festive as the people of Karlsville collected holiday treats and gifts. Behind the counter, Bea wrapped presents in colorful paper, topping them with ribbons and bows. Agatha approached her cautiously. Next to her, Kate began to wiggle with excitement.

"Mama," the girl breathed, her eyes bright.

"Good afternoon," Bea greeted Agatha, but her eyes didn't so much as flicker in her daughter's direction.

"Hmm," Agatha answered. She couldn't come right out and ask

Bea if she could see Kate. It would come across as unhinged. She shifted from foot to foot. "Has everything been. . . all right with you?" she finally asked.

Bea nodded, her face, as always these days, perfectly neutral.

"Mama," Kate repeated, louder this time, but again, Bea showed no reaction. Agatha, sensing the girl's growing distress, winced, and Bea tilted her head.

"Is everything...all right with you?" Bea's hands never stopped wrapping as she spoke, stretching and securing the paper around a large, rectangular box before moving onto the next.

"Quite," Agatha rushed to say. She was the one who the people of Karlsville went to for help with their problems. It made no sense to burden Bea, who was happily oblivious to the ghostly child. The point of all of this had been to protect Bea and keep her happy. If Agatha upset her now, all their work, all their sacrifice, would be for naught. Agatha cleared her throat. "Just needed some sugar for a little holiday baking."

Next to her, Kate had started stomping her little booted feet, her face scrunched up with tears that couldn't fall. But even as her shouts and jerky movements dissolved into a tantrum that rang in Agatha's ears—"Mama, mama, *mama*"—and drowned out the holiday hustle and bustle, nobody in the store reacted. Nobody else could see or hear her. Disconcerted, Agatha shouted a good-bye that was conspicuously loud and rushed home.

Kate spent the rest of the day crumpled on the living room floor, emitting a loud, piercing wail that echoed through the cottage. Agatha tried to comfort the girl, resting her hand on a hot shoulder with a hushed, "There, there," but nothing she did helped. Because, really, how do you soothe a grief over what will never come to be? How could the girl have lost something she never had to begin with?

Bea's mother, Katherine, paid a visit late that afternoon, a fruitcake tucked under her elbow.

"For you," Katherine said as she handed it to Agatha with mittened hands. Agatha stared, trying to ignore the high-pitched keening that bounced off the cottage walls, but it was hard to hear her old friend. When the witch said nothing, Katherine continued. "Bea's doing so much better, and when I asked, she said you'd helped her. Thank you."

Agatha could only make out a few of Katherine's words. Behind her, Kate began to kick her feet and beat the floorboards with her fists. But Katherine, who Kate was presumably named after, just watched Agatha with a quizzical smile, as if Agatha's eardrums weren't on the verge of bursting. Not sure what to say, Agatha nodded—it seemed a safe enough reply—then shut the door in Katherine's face.

It was that night, while Agatha was lying in bed pretending to sleep, that she heard the first *bang*.

Agatha jumped from her bed and ran to the living room, scared about what she'd find, but more scared not to know. Kate sat in the rocking chair again, but this time, instead of staying motionless, the chair swayed, ever so slightly, and the little ghost was staring at her own skinny legs with a look of wonder. Then, screwing up her face into a jumble of rage and hurt and despair—not unlike the howls she'd been releasing since that afternoon—she stretched her legs to the floorboards and gave a mighty push. The chair swung back wildly and hit the wall behind it. Bang!

That's when the nightmare truly began.

Agatha hoped that Kate's interactions with the physical world would tire her, as Agatha had observed with other spirits, but the more Kate practiced, the more adept the little ghost became at touching and moving the objects around her. Kate was not a spirit depleted, hollowed out by decades of living; she had a lifetime's worth of pent-up energy to expend. The rest of the night it was the rocking chair—bang, bang, bang! By the next night she moved onto other objects: Agatha's modest collection of books, the logs at the fireplace, the kitchen chairs—slam, slam, slam! And the night after that, she discovered that she could break things, and the clatter and smash of teacups and bowls and pottery reverberated throughout the once peaceful cottage.

Unsure what else to do, Agatha drove her geese outside, away from the violence of the tiny ghost's fury. She piled their sturdy little lean-to, built by Will Lind, with fresh straw and blankets, and then she retreated into her bedroom. When Kate followed her in and began opening and closing her dresser drawers with a resounding crash, over and over and over, Agatha sought refuge in her closet, where she curled up tight, knees to chest, and sealed her hands over her ringing ears.

Agatha's unusual behavior did not go unnoticed by the people of Karlsville. Their late-night knocks at her cottage door went unanswered, even though they could tell from the cacophony of noise inside that she was home. There were no teas or charms to ease their holiday stress, no syrups or serums for their winter colds, no sagely uttered advice to keep their more minor problems in perspective. Assuming that the witch had bigger, more important things to deal with than their everyday minutiae, they respected her privacy and left her, so they thought, in peace.

It was Lacey Peterson who finally sounded the alarm. Every year, her in-laws descended on her home for holiday festivities. And every year, once Christmas Day wound down and the kids passed out in happy heaps of exhaustion, Lacey snuck out of her overcrowded house and visited Agatha, who knew just the cure for long days with nosy, critical in-laws—a sympathetic ear paired with a generous glass of homemade elderberry wine. When Lacey, bundled in her thick, winter coat, knocked and knocked at Agatha's door that Christmas night, only to be answered with a series of crashes and bangs, she resolved to check in with Will Lind when he got back to town.

Will, who always spent the Christmas holiday with his widowed mother a few towns over, hadn't yet unpacked when Lacey showed up at his door to explain what happened the night before. He didn't bother putting on a show, asking, "Why are you coming to me?" He just thanked Lacey for the information, and as soon as the door closed behind her, he left his dirty travel clothes strewn across his bed and went straight to Agatha's.

If you listen to the town's version of what happened next, Will either ripped Agatha's back door off its hinges or broke a window with his bare hands, staining the pristine snow with his blood. In reality, Will Lind had been warming Agatha's bed for over fifteen years, and he simply used his key to enter her back door.

Agatha, at that point, had barely slept or eaten since winter solstice. She was afraid to leave her cottage. If she did, the spirit of Bea's daughter would follow her, and the objects the little ghost threw and pounded and crashed and slammed would be even more bizarre and frightening to the townsfolk, who couldn't see her, than they were to Agatha. So, Agatha had stayed put, a prisoner in her own home, bone-weary and weak with lack of sleep and food, but unable to rest and too unnerved to eat. Agatha even resorted to bargaining, promising to give up magic altogether—no medicines, no charms, no spells—if her unwanted guest would leave her in peace, but to no avail.

When Will found her, Agatha was in her guest bedroom, shivering under the quilt. He peeled back the covers, prompting Agatha to shriek in terror, but he didn't react as he climbed into bed beside her and pulled the sheets and blankets over both their heads, covering them in darkness.

There was a long moment of silence between the two, filled only with the crash, crash, crash of the closet door slamming. Next to her, Will heaved a resigned sigh, and it occurred to Agatha that she might love him.

"What have you done now, Agatha Franke?"

Five nights ago, when Kate had appeared, Will could have pulled out her fingernails and Agatha wouldn't have confessed to freezing Bea's heart, but she was broken with exhaustion now, and the story spilled out of her. With the exception of a "You did what now?" when she got to the part about Mabel, Will listened without interrupting. When she was done, he squeezed her hand and said, "I'm getting Beatrice."

Agatha wanted to protest. It was Bea, after all, who she'd wanted to protect, to shield from her own heartbreak. But Agatha couldn't go on as she had been, tormented by a ghost whose existence she'd accidentally thwarted. It was untenable, and Agatha may have been stubborn, but she wasn't stupid.

Will left to inform Bea of the situation, then he returned, staying close to Agatha until the sunset and the first rap-rap-rap sounded. Agatha, with Will beside her, opened her front door to Beatrice and Katherine, who didn't wait for an invitation before bustling inside. Will must have prepared them for what they'd find because neither of them flinched at the broken shards of dishes or the books and knickknacks spread across the floor. Neither did they look surprised at Agatha's rumpled clothes and unkempt hair.

"We'll take it from here," Katherine told Will.

Before the door closed behind him, she and Bea were already tidying the cottage, sweeping garbage from the floor, and moving small furniture and other doodads into the bedrooms, so that the living room and kitchen were clear. As they worked, other women of Karlsville trickled in, each of them immediately joining in to clean and organize...Lacey Peterson, of course, who had alerted Will; Heather Schubert, Ernest Karl's ex-wife; Doris Gregg; Rita Lewis; Cassandra Hansen. By the time the main living area was bare and open, a dozen of Agatha's neighbors had gathered. The bangs and clanks of Kate's ghost were contained to the bedrooms, and Agatha's friends reacted to the noises with varying degrees of fear. Heather's eyes shifted nervously every time a particularly loud boom sounded, whereas Cassandra, who had five boys at home, didn't appear to notice the racket. They all, however, stole curious glances at Agatha's icebox as they worked.

Katherine and Bea directed the women to gather in a circle 'round the fireplace. Agatha fell in with the rest, but her stomach was shrinking into a small, dense stone in her guts. Clearly, these women had arrived with the intention of helping, of somehow fixing the predicament Agatha had created, but the truth was that Agatha had no idea how to correct this particular mistake. And even if she had, Kate had ruined all of the ingredients she would have needed. All the plants and herbs and tree barks and flowers she'd spent years collecting with such particular care, had ended up scattered and useless on the cottage floor.

"Thank you, all of you, for coming here tonight," Agatha began, her hands twisting in her apron. "I appreciate it. Truly, I do." This was never in doubt. Everyone knew that Agatha never said anything she didn't mean. "But I don't know how to fix this. I just need to—"

"Agatha." Katherine interrupted her gently, squeezing the witch's fingers in her own. "Let us try. All right?"

Agatha turned to Bea, the one with the most to lose. Agatha had no idea what Bea and her mother had planned, what spell they'd concocted, but there was a real chance it could ruin the peace Beatrice had needed so desperately.

"I'll be fine," Bea assured her. "I needed a break, I think. From the hurt and the—the humiliation—" She was interrupted by a series of murmurs and shaking heads from around the circle. Every heartache feels unique, a burden unborn by others, but the truth is that most people feel its sting at one point or another. "But over the past few weeks, I've been able to step back a bit. To see that he wasn't worth what I was putting myself through."

Across the room, Doris, who was old enough to be Bea's grandmother, muttered, "I always thought he had a weak chin, myself." Everyone, including Beatrice, gave nods and giggles of agreement.

"Besides," Bea added, and her blue eyes flicked to Agatha's bedroom, where it sounded like a chair had just been flipped over, "if it's not too late—and I know it might be, but maybe not—I have to admit I'm curious. To maybe meet my daughter someday."

Agatha nodded, her throat tight, and then the women of Karlsville shocked her by emptying their pockets and revealing a veritable treasure trove of herbs and plants. Juniper and pine for grounding. Basil and cinnamon for cleansing. Mugwort for protection. They landed in the fireplace with a comforting sizzle, and a rich, aromatic smoke filled the living room. It appeared that the women of Karlsville hadn't simply been benefitting from Agatha's knowledge— they'd been learning from it.

Katherine cleared her throat. "I understand that you, Agatha

Franke, have created a ghost of sorts. A little girl who was meant to be, but now will not be, unless things change. Such a spirit is distressing, to say the least—," a loud crash interrupted her here, causing them all to jump. "So we wanted to remind you of the other ghosts you've created with your interference and your magic. I'll start."

Katherine pulled a tiny, knitted set of baby booties from her pocket, cradling them in her palm. "When Bea was born, almost nineteen years ago now, I expected to be elated. Being a wife and mother was, after all, what I'd always wanted. But I didn't feel happy. Not at all. I was exhausted and sore and overwhelmed, and you, Agatha, were the only one who recognized it." Katherine tossed the booties into the fire, and Agatha couldn't contain her gasp of shock. The other women, however, seemed to have expected the gesture. "When I admitted to you how sad I was, how melancholy, you worked tirelessly to help me. For months you made teas, herbal baths, whatever you could think of to help. You even came and cared for Bea so I could take a walk or read a book. I truly don't know what I would have done without you. So tonight, Agatha, I offer the ghost of a young mother. A young mother who may not have survived those early days without your help."

Agatha swallowed hard, blinking back the burn of tears. Katherine met her gaze, her own eyes shining with unshed emotion, and then she said, her voice strong,

"Judge her not by one mistake,
But by the sum of choices, she doth make."

The rest of the women repeated the words, then Heather Schubert stepped forward, who looked to Agatha with a rueful smile. "I'll admit I wasn't thrilled with how publicly you announced Ernest's infidelity." A round of nervous chuckles swept over the circle, and Heather's smile stretched into a grin. "But I can tell you that without it, I would probably still be trapped in that truly awful marriage. It was hard at first, but you were always there to listen when I needed it, and I love the life I have now." Heather had used the money from her divorce settlement to buy and open a restaurant, and it was now Karlsville's most popular eating establishment. Heather held up a dark lock of hair. "It's Karl's. I don't know why I held onto it, but..." She threw it onto the fire. "Tonight, I offer the ghost of a woman who lived her life lonely and unfulfilled because nobody had the courage to tell her the truth."

And then Heather uttered the incantation, with the other women following,

"Judge her not by one mistake,

But by the sum of choices, she doth make."

One by one, the offerings continued, moving around the circle. Some of the stories brought smiles—the courage tea Agatha made for Rita when she was starring in the town play and was convinced she'd vomit on stage from nerves, whereas others evoked tears—herbs and charms to soothe debilitating grief after the deaths of parents and spouses. Precious objects—love letters, handmade lace and drops of expensive perfume—found their way into the flames, tokens of gratitude for a witch who had forever changed, mostly for the better, the town she loved so much.

During one tense moment, Cassandra tried to sacrifice her son's pet gerbil. "Dammit, I thought I'd be able to get rid of it here! Honest to Pete, he's only had him two days and it's already leaving droppings all over the house." However, the nervous-looking rodent was rescued by Agatha, who knew that was a kind of magic she would no longer be dabbling in.

By the time it was Beatrice's turn, the crashes and bangs from the bedroom had ceased, and only the quiet murmur of voices remained. Bea looked at the circle of women around her, women who had survived all manner of pain and fear and sadness, and scrubbed a hand over her tear-streaked cheeks. Agatha didn't have to check the icebox to know that the small heart tucked inside was no longer frozen. And that, Agatha knew, was a gift. Heartache, no matter how painful, wasn't simply a cost of being human, it was an essential part of it. It had been a disservice to take that away from Beatrice, no matter how well intentioned.

"I'm sorry." Beatrice turned to Agatha, her tears falling freely now. "I'm sorry for pushing you to perform that spell. You knew better, but you were afraid for me. I promise I'm going to be all right." Bea held up a small paper envelope. "This is the first charm I made with you. I was scared before my first day of school, and you let me help you pick out the flowers and herbs. I've always cherished it because it reminded me of you, and I hoped that, one day, I might have a little touch of your magic." The packet hit the fire, one final sacrifice, and when the women chanted the incantation, their skirts rustled and twisted as the front door flew open and banged into the stone wall.

A breeze flew through the room, frigid at first. Cold enough to freeze. The women hugged themselves and huddled close to each other for warmth. Then the air burned hot and arid. Sweat broke out on their brows, and wide-eyed, they huddled even closer together, this time out of fear. At that point, Agatha felt a gentle touch along her back, a tentative stroke of tiny fingers as the uninvited spirit rushed toward the door, and Agatha knew it was only a matter of time until their paths crossed once again. Under much happier circumstances, of course. Finally, the wind gentled, and the little cottage was neither cold nor hot. It was just her familiar, cozy home again.

That night, after everyone left, Agatha washed, ate, and crawled into bed, tired and relieved. Will was waiting for her, and for once, Agatha didn't pretend to be annoyed by his presence. She snuggled into the comforting heat of his shoulder, her mind replaying the stories her friends had shared. It might have gone to a witch's head, but Agatha knew better than to gloss over how badly she'd botched the situation with Bea. It was a grave mistake she'd made, and in the process, she'd lost Mabel.

Still, Agatha mused, overall, it appeared her contributions had been more good than bad.

Will's arm tightened around her, and Agatha smiled into his chest. Then, as he always did, Will leaned down and kissed her forehead.

"Marry me."

As she always did, Agatha opened her mouth to turn him down. But tonight, she paused. She'd just listened to a lot of stories about ghosts. Life was littered with them, ghosts of lives unlived. The ghosts of good decisions and bad decisions, easy and hard decisions. For every choice made, another choice went unpursued, and for the first time, Agatha wondered what ghosts she was leaving in her wake. Somewhere out there, was one of her ghosts married to Will? She took a moment to consider it. That ghost probably had her fair share of gripes and complaints. Dirty boots in the house. A mother-in-law who might not be keen to share her son. Extra laundry. But if she was honest, and Agatha was always honest, she suspected that it probably wasn't all bad. That ghost fell asleep every night cocooned in Will's strong arms. She shared tea with him around the fire in the evening and chatted with him about her day. She walked openly down the street with him, arm in arm. That ghost was probably, Agatha had to admit, quite happy.

With a quiet hum, Agatha pretended to debate her answer, and Will grew still beside her. It was the first time she hadn't immediately rejected him. Then she patted his cheek and closed her eyes.

"Maybe."

Captain Cobra
rara ratbag

He's the world's greatest Sadist
her biggest weakness, see
He fosters her monster
and knows how to defeat it—
Then eat it.

It hurts so good
she's addicted,
Yet conflicted
For how He's depicted—
As a Monster.

He's not cautious,
she's nauseous from overthinking.
He's easy to read
If she picks up the seeds
And plants them in her mind.

It's the s p a c e s in between
Where she feels seen
Those rare moments of grace
He loses His poker face
And spills the hot tea.

Its burning,
she's yearning for answers.
So lap up that tea, evil one,
And you'll know His true nature—
the full picture few get to see.

They Try

R. Minter

The first time I saw it, we were rattling down a country road toward the town of Sycamore. Well, technically not the first, but the first time in years.

Steve and Terry were arguing in the back. After a token resistance, I'd retired to the passenger seat and surrendered the wheel to David. Four harbingers of science and logic hurtling after their next paycheck in a bone-white van.

As the leader, I claim dominance over the reins of our steed. Usually. The last few nights I had been lacking in sleep. After nearly running into a tree a few miles back when my eyelids drooped, David had put his foot down.

Now I was stuck staring out the passenger side window, watching a dense forest in all its autumn colors slide by. My vision blurred as fatigue took its toll.

That's when it happened.

Something appeared, keeping pace with spindly limbs too large in the back, too short in the front. To my eyes, it was little more than a gray blur with a bulbous head. It slid between the almost non-existent shoulder of the road, flailing in an off-kilter gait.

The vestiges of lucidity tried to make it into a man racing on all fours. The small, insane voice, born of the space in between waking and sleep, giggled. That's not a man. They don't really know what people are supposed to look like, but they try.

The not-a-man's head turned.

I jerked upright with a shout.

David echoed me, yanking on the wheel as he jumped.

For a second, my heart stopped. The van skidded sideways on

the loose gravel. My brain grappled with the idea of getting smeared on a tree as the utter wrongness of what I'd seen in the running man's face faded like the afterimage of a camera flash.

My pulse hammered to life again. David wrestled the van back where it belonged, and the sleep-addled imprint melted away.

A string of curses came from all three of my team.

"Seriously, Michelle? Are you trying to get us killed today?" David said through gritted teeth.

My face grew hot. "Sorry. Bad dreams."

"Don't you have meds for that?" Terry asked from behind me. I could practically hear the sneer.

"No, Terry. My therapist and I both agreed to try without them for a couple of weeks. I haven't had issues in a long time."

"Except, apparently, when you're not on your meds. I think all of us would appreciate not having heart attacks every time you have a scary dream."

I didn't grace her with a response. My therapist had assured me the first week would be rough, but so help me, I was going to push through. I'd just had my thirty-second birthday, for God's sake. Time to learn how not to be afraid of imaginary things.

"You try the meditation track I sent you?"

Ah, Steve. The mom of the group. I'd certainly pushed his patience over the last few days, yet his temper remained unflappable.

I patted the phone in my jeans pocket. "Sure did. Helped me get to sleep. It's just the after that's still rough."

"Hmm." He went quiet, no doubt percolating a new plan to soothe his toddler of a teammate.

"It's the after that's rough for us, too," Terry mumbled.

I sighed and returned to watching the now running-man-free scenic view out my window.

* * *

The outer edge of Sycamore had an odd sight of its own. Tents. A dozen in sight and probably more nestled further out in the forest. Each tent had at least one vehicle nearby, all haphazardly splayed out among the trees.

"Like pilgrims coming to a holy site," David said with a shake of his head.

I scoffed. "More like flies to a corpse."

"Or four," Terry added with far more enthusiasm than

necessary.

I shrugged. "Either way, looks like our timing is right."

"Well, everyone knows supernaturals and extraterrestrials fear the light," Steve said, before pointing over my shoulder. Two police trucks flanked the road to Sycamore. A pair of police officers stood beside each vehicle, the early morning sun glinting off of their guns. "The police, on the other hand, probably enjoy the easier targeting."

"Fair. David, drive up slowly. They look kind of on edge."

We didn't get much farther before four pistols pointed in our direction. David slammed on the brakes and threw his hands in the air.

"Hey, is that legal?" Terry asked.

I snorted, exuding bravado to cover up the jump in my breathing as I reached for the door handle. "Will it matter when we're full of holes?" Much to the dismay of my teammates, I slipped out of the van and pointed my own hands toward the sky. "Michelle Moore, from *Fact Hunters*. We had an appointment, I believe?"

I tried to keep my voice loud enough to cover the forty feet between us and the cops, but also level, a hard thing to do when you're one trigger pull away from dead.

One cop lowered his gun and grinned. "Ms. Moore! Sorry, I didn't recognize you at first! I really need to get new contacts." He holstered his weapon and motioned for his buddies to do the same. "Relax, these guys are here to help."

Their grimaces as they put their pistols away told me they weren't so sure. If I wanted the job to go well, I needed to change that. I dropped my hands, squared my shoulders, plastered on my best professional smile, and marched up to them like I dealt with this kind of thing all the time. If I was honest, I did.

I pointed toward the tent city at their border. "Looks like you've got squatters. Happens a lot with unexplained cases, especially when they happen in clusters."

A policewoman, who looked capable of chewing nails, glared at me. "Fantastic. If you're here to help, I assume you're going to get rid of them."

"That's exactly what I intend to do, Officer . . ."

She filled the space with more glaring.

I coughed. "Yes. As I was saying, I intend to do just that. My team and I are here to prove once and for all that *nothing* paranormal or extraterrestrial happened to your people."

"Your team, the ones still in the van?"

I glanced back. Sure enough, no one had moved. I sighed. "Yes, them. They're a little gun shy."

Officer Nails frowned.

The wispy policeman next to her chuckled. "Apologies, Ms. Moore. We've had a lot of problems with our new guests. So obsessed with the supernatural, they've got no respect for the dead."

"Or the living," Nails growled.

The cop who had grinned at me stepped up, getting awfully close to my personal bubble. He was still grinning. "Don't mind them, they don't know what you're capable of. I do, though." He rubbed the back of his neck. "I'm a huge fan, Ms. Moore. I've watched all of *Fact Hunters* at least a dozen times."

My eyes widened. "A . . . dozen? Wow."

After struggling in its first couple of years, our show had gained a number of dedicated watchers. Still, the idea of it having so avid a fan took me by surprise.

He puffed out his chest and stuck out his hand. "Officer Nichols, at your service."

I shook his hand, giving him a conspiratorial look. "Am I to assume you're the reason we're here?"

"You assume correct. The Chief officially hired you, but I knew just who to call after the loonies showed up."

"Hey, the Chief wants to talk to them." The fourth cop, who had slipped away while I was preoccupied, waved from out the window of a police truck.

"Oh, right! This way, ma'am." Nichols' grin warped, pulling the corners of his mouth up, up, up, crawling along his cheekbones as gums gave way to bone.

My breath caught, and it was gone. No bone, no overstretched mouth. Just a young cop with a giddy expression.

I let out a nervous giggle. A hallucination brought on by stress and lack of sleep, nothing more. Suddenly, I regretted not bringing my pills. "Uh, can I get the rest of my team, or am I the only one invited?"

Nichols blushed. "Oh, no, not just you. By all means, uh, bring your van, too. We'll let it through. You'll need all your stuff, anyway."

"Yes, we will."

I turned and walked off, forcing my legs to stay below a run as my professional facade threatened to drop. His twisted face stayed clear in my mind. I'd taken the last of my pills right before I got a call from Sycamore's Chief of Police, and I'd refused a refill knowing I'd take them if given half the chance. If I'd known about this job beforehand, I'd have never stopped.

* * *

After a painfully dull time spent going over what we were and were not allowed to do, as well as a brief burst of excitement as we convinced Terry that insulting the police Chief was a terrible idea, Officer Nichols led us to the first place of death.

It happened in a ranch house near the center of town. Its occupant, a single, moderately wealthy artist, had fled city life a few years prior. Sycamore's middle-of-nowhere aesthetic had "pulled her in like a magnet," or so Nichols told us. Looking inside her home, I had to wonder when she lamented her decision.

The smell hit first, acrid and coppery, the air heavy with a dash of decay and salt. Remnants of her old life remained. Bright paintings on the wall, cherry-wood desks on top of lush, blue carpet. Then came the sights.

Used up candles of myriad colors littered nearly every inch of floor space. I couldn't fathom how the house hadn't burned down. Circles of salt, now smudged into oblong messes, worked their way from the living room, down the hallway, and into the bathroom.

I paused at the threshold, a curtain of dread falling over me. *Leave*, the primal part of my brain demanded. Some things are better left alone.

I ignored it. It was hardly the first time I'd felt trepidation on a case.

"These cameras aren't light, you know."

David's voice startled the hesitation out of me. I moved aside, muttering an apology.

Terry and Steve followed with more gear. Laptops, recorders, EMF gauges, microphones. To anyone who didn't know us, they'd think we were more ghost hunters looking to capitalize on Sycamore's misfortune. But sometimes you had to fight fire with fire.

I'd grown a career from taking all the tricks of paranormal investigators and turning them on their creators. Where they saw souls in pictures, I proved backscatter. Where they saw floating apparitions, I proved smoke and mirrors.

My team was a streamlined machine. They scattered with little input from me, setting up equipment in obvious hotspots.

I turned to Officer Nichols, who stood nearby, gazing at me with puppy-dog eyes. "The victim, Ms. Campbell, passed away in the bathroom, correct?"

He'd filled us in on the way over, but I preferred hearing it at the scene itself.

"Yes. Lying, fully clothed, in the bathtub." He frowned. "It looked like she'd taken a nap. Peaceful, hands at her sides. Had a horrible grin on her face, though."

I tensed. "A grin?"

"A Cheshire Cat looking one. According to Theo, her jaw was clenched so tight, some of her teeth broke. He said it had to do with rigor mortis. Either way, it didn't look right."

"I see." I relaxed a little. Muscle spasms after death did odd things to bodies. Completely normal. "Theo is Sycamore's coroner?"

"Yes. He's been here since I was a kid."

Which meant at least fifteen years. Surely a man capable of invaluable insight. "I'll have to make sure to speak with him tomorrow. For now, I'd like to check out that bathroom."

"Oh, of course." Nichols motioned for me to go first. "Don't worry about the salt and stuff. We've cataloged what we need, and the loonies have already messed up a lot, anyway."

Even with his okay, I tiptoed around as much as I could. It just seemed right. "I'm surprised the *enthusiasts* haven't taken all of this for their collections." A common act among the fanatics—and Officer Nails had responded like she'd been dealing with fanatics.

"Oh, they've taken a lot. There was just so much to start."

"When did Ms. Campbell become interested in the occult?"

"Well, the week before her death, although 'interested' isn't the word I'd use."

"What word would you use?"

"Terrified. She called the station every night, claimed shadows were stalking her."

Blood rushed to my ears as I entered the bathroom, drowning out his voice. The world shrank to the thing before me.

Long, black tendrils rose from the bathtub, whipping in the air as an overwhelming smell of death emanated from it. They spun and sucked downward, disappearing down the drain with the sound of a hundred insect legs.

"We looked multiple times—"

I motioned for Nichols to stop talking, not daring to take my eyes off the drain. "Did you see that?"

"See what?"

"In the tub." My brain ran circles, trying to pin down a rational reason for what I'd seen. Three hallucinations in a matter of hours was a new record, even for me. "Are there rodents here, or bugs?"

"Probably. We live next to a forest." Nichols eased himself past me, hand covering his mouth and nose as he entered the bathroom. "I don't see anything. I'd like to know what you think about that, though." He pointed at the floor.

I dragged my mind back to the job at hand, vowing to call my therapist as soon as I could.

Dried blood sketched a pentacle across tan tiles, a single point facing toward the door, two points facing the bathtub in the back. Each line was immaculate. Roughly half an inch thick, each edge looked sharp enough to cut. A perfect crimson circle contained the star, while a thin strip of ragged cloth lay in the center.

Not a smudge of dirt blemished the rest of the floor. "What kind of blood is that?"

Nichols shrugged before retreating into the hallway. "Don't know. Our lab couldn't tell us. We had some sent out of town, but the results won't be back for a few more days."

I stepped out of the bathroom. The smell fell away, returning to the more mild burn and death of the rest of the place. Strange. I'd have to give the room special attention. "It's probably a mixture of different animals' blood. That can throw off tests."

"Yeah, I suppose so. What do you think of that star, though?"

"The pentacle? Could mean a lot of things, although the blood makes me think of darker intentions. At first glance? I'd say either Ms. Campbell desperately wanted attention, or someone played a horrible trick on her."

Nichols' eyes narrowed, his demeanor morphing from star-struck guide to skeptical law enforcement. "Ms. Moore, there's no evidence of homicide, and dying seems an odd way to get attention."

"Many originally 'unexplained' deaths are accidental consequences of desperate acts." I marched back toward the living room as the logical explanations of what really could have happened solidified in my mind.

I gestured grandly to the candles littering the floor, gaining a sidelong look from David as he appeared from the kitchen. "For instance, these candles all create carbon monoxide. A few won't do harm, but a truckload? That's a recipe for disaster."

I took a deep breath, ready to launch into my next scenario.

A woman burst through the front door, a ragged scarf flapping around her neck and a patchwork jacket two sizes too large hanging from her slight frame.

She moved with unexpected speed, closing the distance between us so quickly that I found myself staring into her wild, bloodshot eyes before I could blink. My stomach dropped.

"She saw. She *believed*. They all did." Her breath washed over me, a caustic mix of tooth decay and hard liquor. "If you believe, you must know. Better to not believe than die."

Nichols imposed an arm between me and the new arrival, pushing her to a more comfortable distance. "Margaret, you've been drinking again." He pitched his voice as if talking to a child. "You're an adult, and you're allowed to, but please stop accosting people while you're at it."

Margaret sidestepped Nichols with a grace unseen in the inebriated. I locked eyes with her a second time, my confidence failing me as the situation stirred an eerily similar memory.

A towering, crazed lady, her height exaggerated to my eight-year-old self. I'd cowered behind my mother, tears streaming down my face, as my father held the lady back. Her antics drove the horror of the previous day's ordeal to new peaks.

"You see. You believe!" she'd cried, jabbing a bony finger toward me. "You must know! If you don't, they do. They come in the in-between. They hunt. They take."

I was no longer eight, my trial nearly two decades behind me, yet still I trembled under Margaret's stare. "They know, they know! Why don't you?"

After threats from Nichols and a descent into even more incoherent rambling from Margaret, she blustered out of the house, leaving me to shiver.

"You okay?" Steve put his hand on my shoulder.

All of my team had gathered to see the show as their boss got harassed by the local drunk.

I took a deep breath, fought the urge to gag on the thick air, and demanded my body to stop shaking like a chihuahua. "Yes. I'm fine, Steve."

I pushed his hand away and stepped out of the house. I'd come here to debunk the crap happening in the town, not get wrapped up in the hype. Currently, I was failing. I told myself my sour mood was because of my poor work performance, yet it did nothing to dull the feeling that all I wanted was to finish the job and leave.

* * *

The second mysterious death in the town of Sycamore involved a teenage resident who'd gone out to purchase groceries. He'd left at five in the evening.

A churchgoer had found him two days later in the church courtyard, draped over a rock mound which hadn't existed the day before. They described him as looking "peacefully asleep." Stranger still, he'd only been wearing an old, ragged, business suit that wasn't his. His clothes—and undergarments—had vanished. No fingerprints, no blood, nothing to suggest murder or a cause of death beyond the fact he no longer lived.

The suit caught my eye, but I kept my hunch to myself until I viewed the third and last scene of death.

That one involved human blood—and a lot of it. According to another resident, an elderly couple had decided to take a walk on the banks of the town's creek. Odd all by itself, Nichols assured me, since the creek stood a mile away from their residence and both had back problems. Normally, they rarely left their house at all. Still, the witness claimed to watch them walk off spritely enough and had thought little else of it.

A child had stumbled onto the remains. I couldn't still the roiling in my gut as I looked across the blood-soaked leaves gathered along the riverbank.

Nichols told me the couple was already dead when the child spotted them, but were they really? I could envision another child walking into a bloody scene, watching in horror as a man succumbed to a fate so twisted, so wrong, not even deep hypnosis could tease the truth from the depth of the child's fractured mind.

I swallowed the bile in the back of my throat, glad I hadn't stopped for lunch. "This looks like a crime scene."

"Yeah, I think I'll set up the perimeter," Terry said as she tiptoed around the macabre splatter painted across a large swath of the riverbank. "I just got new shoes."

Steve and David grumbled about being forced further into the mess. I couldn't blame them. Blood covered the area, but that wasn't all.

Chunks of matter peeked from above and below leaves and detritus, filling the air with the smell of rotting flesh.

I cocked my head, studying the scene. Other than the bustle of my team, it was quiet, still. In another time and place, it would have been tranquil. Here, it sent a chill up my spine. "Why aren't there any signs of animals? Where are the insects, the flies?"

I cast my question at Nichols, who had taken up vigil about twenty feet away. The sour look on his face he'd adopted since arriving at the scene deepened. "Don't know. It's all . . . Uh . . . from Mr. and Mrs. Lancaster. We collected the... bigger remains, but didn't have a good way of cleaning the rest. Figured the forest critters would help, but . . ."

There had to be a logical explanation. I tapped my chin. There was always a logical explanation. "Chemicals."

"Ms. Moore?"

"Were the remains tested for chemicals? Maybe someone sprayed the area to keep animals away."

"Nothing came up, same as everything else. There's no blood unaccounted for, and no signs of a struggle."

I raised an eyebrow. "How could you tell?"

Nichols went pale. "Theo said it was all self-inflicted."

"Exactly what was self-inflicted?"

"The . . . cuts. Both sliced bits off their arms and legs all the way to the bone." His pallor gained a green tinge. "I don't know how they lived long enough to do it. Then they showed up dead, looking like they'd laid down to sleep."

"Thank you, that's enough."

He looked about to pass out, and I wasn't sure I wanted the only person around with a weapon to be incapacitated. Still, there was one thing I had to know. "What about their clothes? Did they still have theirs?"

"Clothes? Uh . . . yeah. They had them, but they were laid on top of their bodies like blankets, and they were off."

I latched onto the word, a tiny voice in the back of my mind equal parts intrigued and appalled.

"Parts were bigger than they should be, or smaller. Mr. Lancaster's left sleeve wasn't big enough for a kid, yet his left pant leg could have fit two of him. Mrs. Lancaster's dress was worse. It looked crumpled, but when I looked closer, it was because some threads were tiny, some were huge."

The tiny voice lost its intrigue and cried in alarm. I tamped it down. "Anything else? Anything that wasn't theirs?"

"A—a hat. At least, I think it was supposed to be a hat. Found it right in the center of it all, clean as a whistle. Looked like it'd been made from really old, torn up cloth, just big enough for a doll."

My mind snapped to a particular person, one who was practically a walking storefront for ragged, torn clothing. "Did all the victims talk to Margaret before their accidents?"

"Probably."

The nonchalance in his tone caught me off-guard. "And you don't find it odd that you found ragged bits of clothing near every victim, and these victims also talked to Margaret?"

Nichols shook his head. "I understand how it looks to an outsider, but everyone in this town talks, or at least is talked to, by Margaret pretty much every day. It's like saying they all died from eating."

"You don't find the clothes strange at all?"

"Oh, I find them plenty strange. But nothing's turned up on any of them. Not even a hair."

Something flickered at the edge of my sight. I turned toward it. A camera stood on a tripod on the other side of the splattered ground. A large shadow moved behind it. I tried to make it into Terry, Steve, or David.

As if spurred on by my attention, it leaned out, staring at me as I stared at it.

Wrong was the first thought to form. The thing stood on two mismatched legs, a crooked, bloated torso balanced precariously on top. Its arms and head were no less off. Its features shifted and distorted as if looking into a cruel funhouse mirror. One of its eyes bulged from its misshapen head, growing in size until it appeared on the verge of popping. It opened swollen lips, mouthing silent words which burrowed into my being.

You see. You believe.

Ice rushed through my veins. I was back in my place of birth, a small country town with a crazy lady of its own and a series of mysterious deaths. My eight-year-old self stumbled upon a shadow as it towered over a writhing man. The man contorting, shifting, screaming in agony until all that remained was the wrongness.

"Ms. Moore, are you okay? You're a bit pale."

Nichols' words cut through my panic, the shadow from my past and present gone.

"I . . ." My heart hammered against my breastbone, a light whine in my ears. A quick glance showed Nichols wasn't the only person looking at me with concern.

My teammates' eyes bore into me. Terry's in particular seemed to scream "I told you so." Going off my meds had been a terrible idea. Refusing to carry extra, doubly so.

"Ms. Moore?"

"No, Officer Nichols, I'm not." A weight descended at the admission, threatening to crush me. "I think it would be best if I postponed my investigation."

"You've got to be kidding me," Terry said from my left. "We came all the way out to the middle of nowhere, spent half the day setting up, and now you're quitting?"

I grimaced. "I'm not saying we're quitting. Just give me a couple of days. I trust you guys to gather data while I'm . . . indisposed. When I'm ready, I'll parse the data all day and night if you want."

"No!" Terry jabbed a finger at me. "We've seen enough of you off sleep. Go get your head on straight. We'll pick up your slack."

After an awkward conversation with Nichols, during which I could see his remaining awe for me shrivel and die, and an equally awkward conversation with Steve about how he was glad I was putting my health first, Steve and I arrived at our lodging.

With no such thing as an inn in Sycamore, we'd been given the only empty house in living condition. It was also the home of the late Mr. and Mrs. Lancaster. Originally, I'd been thrilled. Lodging in the house of two of the victims gave me more time to debunk the alien and paranormal fanatics' ridiculous notions.

Now, as Steve pulled out of the gravel driveway, leaving me alone in the front of the red brick two-story house, all I could feel was deep unease. If a townsperson had jumped out and said *boo*, I'd have died of fright. As it stood, the block was eerily still.

So it stayed into the cozy living room, up the well-dusted stairs, and into the perfectly kept guest room.

There I was, in an old-fashioned chair at an old-fashioned writing desk. I intended to call my doctor immediately upon getting here, yet now that I was settled, I find the package of sleeping pills Steve gave me calling my name.

"A nap might do you some good," he'd said.

He's right, I think. Even if the "nap" must be brought on with sedatives.

I downed two small white pills with a glass of water, then added a third for good measure.

They kicked in faster than expected.

I was barely on the bed before the room tilted and fuzzed at the edges, soft but unwelcoming.

The silk inside a coffin.

A giggle sounds at the reaches of my hearing. Or is it? There's something off about it.

Some *wrongness.*

Am I asleep? I can't tell.

Shadows now, congregating around the bed.

Shadows? People?

They watch, they stare, coming almost in focus, then back out again. Not unlike the morphing of their features.

No, not people.

More giggles, inside out.

Mouths grin, backwards.

You see, you believe! You see, you believe! They chant in silence as their arms stretch toward me.

Not people, not people, the mad voice in my head squeals. *They don't know what people are supposed to look like, but they try.*

Brews & Books

Melissa Sasina

)))❂(((

Somehow she'd never noticed it before, the small little cafe on the Square nestled between the old firehouse and the popcorn shop. Charlotte Hazelwood was almost certain that space had never existed, yet it blended in seamlessly with the other Victorian-style buildings surrounding it. Large planters filled with moss and wild violets flanked the door and a wooden sign announced the cafe was called Brews & Books.

She stood there a moment and stared at the door. It really was a strange thing. Medina wasn't a large city like Cleveland or Columbus. If the cafe was new, she'd have heard about it, especially with it being on the historic Square. If it'd been there all along, she would have noticed it in passing. After all, she'd lived in this town for many years and often frequented the Square. And yet, there it stood as if it'd been there forever.

The soft sound of chimes reached her ears.

Charlotte blinked and looked around to realize she stood inside the cafe at the counter. When did she walk inside? Had her feet moved on their own? A frown crossed her face as she tried to remember only to be greeted with a certain fogginess that she couldn't quite shake off. The gentle melody of music filled her ears, soft and almost otherworldly. It lulled away the anxiousness she'd felt before finding the cafe, soothing her.

"Good afternoon."

She had to tilt her head back slightly to meet the green eyes of the baristo who smiled at her and waited. An odd sensation rushed through Charlotte, a cold prickle that raced up her back and made the hairs on her neck stand. The need to place her order and leave whispered in her mind. She glanced quickly at the menu and selected a simple chai latte. Perfect for the chilly autumn morning.

"May I have your name?"

Charlotte opened her mouth to speak, but hesitated.

Don't, something said within her. *A name can be taken.*

The baristo, Basil as his nametag claimed, tilted his head to the side and asked again with a smile, "May I have your name?"

The urge to give him her name was strong, and she battled against it, which was difficult when he spoke so sweetly to her. Far sweeter than *he* did. She frowned. Who was he? She couldn't remember. Ah, the baristo was still waiting for her name.

Don't give your name.

Charlotte decided to offer him a name close enough. "Charlie."

Basil's smile broadened as he grabbed a cup and wrote the name down. "Such a pity. That's not your name," he said, his voice as sweet as honey. "I just wanted to get to know you." He turned away to make the drink.

Charlotte looked around the cafe while she waited and hummed along to the music. It was a simple little place with an old wooden floor that creaked and groaned with each step taken. Plants seemed to consume a majority of the cafe. They climbed the walls, hung from the tin ceiling tiles, even adorned the small bloodwood tables.

However, it was the wall of books that caught her eye. The shelves towered well above her head and were filled with old books that called to her. She reached a hand out, wanting to stroke the spines and run her fingers along pages that were most likely yellowed with age. The thought crossed her mind to pick one and sit down with it at the table. To take long slow sips from her drink as she slowly turned the pages . . .

Don't touch them.

Charlotte withdrew her hand but did not move away from the books. The pull they had on her was greater than anything she'd felt before. She wanted to surround herself with them, to flip through the pages and take in their unique scent. She wanted . . .

"Go ahead. Take one."

His voice broke the hold the books had on her. Charlotte turned to Basil and shook her head. "I appreciate the offer, but not today," she said. There was a tingling that ran through her spine when the words left her mouth, as if she'd made a promise she shouldn't have.

The baristo merely smiled as he held her drink out to her. When had he come to stand beside her? "Perhaps another day," he told her, his hand brushing her own as she took the cup.

Charlotte said nothing, only gave a small nod and stepped through the door.

She was there again, standing outside Brews & Books. How she'd gotten there, Charlotte didn't know. Rain pattered down softly on her umbrella as she contemplated opening the door. The day after her first visit, she'd walked back up to the Square in search of the cafe only to find it was not there. There was no storefront between the old firehouse and popcorn store. Her hand tightened on the umbrella handle. It didn't exist, yet there she was, once more standing in front of the coffee shop. For some reason, she wasn't surprised it had reappeared on a day she felt incredibly down.

The low rumble of thunder mingled with the gentle chime Charlotte now associated with the cafe reached her ears. Once more, she stood before the counter, unsure of when or how she stepped inside. Basil stood behind the counter just as he had done the week before, a smile lighting up his face as if he knew that she'd return.

"What would you like today?"

Charlotte considered the menu briefly before she decided upon a hot apple cider.

"We have samples today," Basil said, pushing a small plate across the counter toward her.

She looked down at the pieces of muffin being offered. They looked absolutely delicious. Ah, was that a blueberry one she saw? Her fingers twitched. There was no harm in just trying one, right? Just one tiny little bite . . .

You could take one, but at what cost?

Charlotte clenched her hand slightly and shook her head. "I appreciate the offer, but I've already eaten." After the last time, she decided that she needed to choose her words carefully. She wasn't sure why, only that it was a feeling that kept tugging at her—a warning that whispered in the back of her mind. *Be careful with your words and don't accept anything that could be considered a gift.*

Basil's smile didn't falter. "Pity." He withdrew the plate and asked, "May I have your name?"

"Charlie," she replied, repeating the same lie as before.

He wrote the name on the cup and turned away.

Charlotte was once again drawn to the wall of books. Their pull on her was still strong as she walked slowly past them, her eyes skimming the titles. Most were faded beyond readability, while others almost seemed to shimmer in the want of attention. And Charlotte was so incredibly tempted to take one in hand and dive into whatever mysteries waited for her within. Her love for books was great and the desire to explore them nearly overwhelming.

"You can take one, if you'd like."

Basil stood beside her with a steaming cup of cider in his hands. When had he gotten there? She hadn't even noticed his approach. Just like before, he seemed to pop up out of nowhere.

Charlotte smiled and said, "Another time." She felt the promise brush against her skin as the words left her mouth. Really, the books could easily be her downfall if she was not careful.

He did not show any disappointment as she took her drink. Only offered her the same sweet smile. Charlotte noticed for the first time that the faintest of dimples appeared when he smiled, and for a brief moment, she thought he was rather cute.

Do not be lured by the beauty of his glamour.

Charlotte shook the thought from her mind. With a smile of unspoken thanks, she turned and walked to the door.

When her hand touched the old brass knob to leave, his voice spoke softly in her ear, "Until next time."

As she walked home, Charlotte could have sworn she was being followed by a raven.

Charlotte shielded her eyes from the brightness of the sun as she looked up at the green and gold sign for Brews & Books. Funny how on all days, when she was feeling completely down and a mess of anxiety, she once more found herself at the cafe. There was a slight tug on her jeans by her ankle, and she glanced down to find a raven looking up at her. Did Ohio even have ravens? Perhaps it was a crow. She wasn't familiar enough with them to be able to tell the difference.

The inky aviator flew up to perch on one of the lampposts along the sidewalk. It watched her, almost curiously, before it cracked its long beak and gave her a low croak.

"Should I?" Charlotte asked in thought with a quick glance at the door.

Shifting on the post, the raven offered her a sort of warbling sound in answer followed by what almost sounded like a giggle, as if it was amused with her hesitation.

"Hmm." She looked back at the door, studying it for the first time. The weathered wooden panels and elaborate carvings spoke of great history which had been painstakingly preserved. The stained glass panes were embellished with a floral pattern. It gave a strangely inviting feeling.

Charlotte didn't even have a chance to touch the doorknob before the familiar chime reached her ears, and she found herself at the counter with Basil smiling at her. She no longer questioned how she ended up inside; she was just happy to see his smile. Especially after the day she'd had.

"What will you be having today?" Basil asked.

Charlotte took a moment to genuinely look over the menu for the first time. At first, it seemed as if it had the standard offerings most coffee shops had, but then the words seemed to blur and shift. Things she didn't like vanished from the menu and were replaced with her favorites. The chalk vines and flowers embellishing the edges of the chalkboard menu fluttered as if they were in a breeze. She blinked and shook her head. No, she must be imagining things. All the stress she'd been dealing with was messing with her head. She should order her drink and go home to rest.

"I'll have an iced chai latte today," she said.

Basil nodded and grabbed a cup, writing her name on it. "We have more samples today," he offered, his eyes glancing down to the plate before returning to her.

Charlotte shook her head. "I appreciate the offer, but I don't feel much like eating today." It wasn't a lie. She hadn't felt like eating much the past few days after dealing with *him*. Ah, but who was he again? She couldn't remember, just as she couldn't remember ever actually walking through the cafe door. How did she get inside again? When had she even walked up to the Square in the first place?

With the shake of her head, she turned away from the counter. Once again, the books called out to her, but this time Charlotte resisted them. Instead, she walked around to look more closely at the plants—and there were quite a few of them.

The delicate velvety petals of one plant in particular caught her attention. The soft lavender, with long ruffled edges and flecks of gold, was beyond anything she'd ever seen. The scent it gave off was like the mingling of a gentle rainy day in a lush meadow—sweet with a hint of earthiness.

Tiny speckled mushrooms dotted the soil around the stem of the flower, seemingly taking refuge beneath its wide leaves. Freckled brown caps sat on stout white stalks that were circled by skirt-like ruffles at the base.

Charlotte leaned closer to get a better look.

One of the mushrooms shifted away from her to duck bashfully behind a leaf. Another more curious mushroom moved close to the edge of the pot. The soft sound of childish laughter bounced around Charlotte.

This isn't normal.

Charlotte backed away quickly and blinked. The mushrooms were perfectly still. Had they really moved? She frowned. No, they couldn't have. They were just mushrooms, after all. It wasn't like they had legs and could walk about. Perhaps she was more sleep deprived than she thought. Maybe she should have gotten a strong dose of coffee instead of a chai.

Charlotte shook her head in an attempt to clear it. The laughter seemed to linger in the back of her mind.

"Are you okay?"

She turned to find Basil once again having materialized suddenly beside her with her drink in hand. He watched her with his head tilted slightly to the side, his usual smile not quite as bright as she remembered it being—almost as if he actually was worried about her.

"I'll be fine," Charlotte said as she took her drink. "I have to be."

He asked no further questions, only smiled at her.

She gave him a slight nod to part ways and headed out the door.

The raven followed her home.

Charlotte wasn't surprised to be outside the cafe. She'd actually come to expect it anymore. Munin, the name she had chosen for the raven, waited for her on the lamppost as he usually did. Her arrival to the coffee shop had gone from once a week, to nearly every day now. She didn't know why she felt so safe there, despite everything in the back of her head continuously warning her to be cautious. Still, the baristo never treated her like *he* did. Basil never hurt her with lies and anger.

Munin warbled at her with an amused tone as he greeted her in his usual manner. The raven always followed her home and seemed to watch over her until nightfall, but once morning arrived, he was nowhere to be seen until she arrived at the shop.

"Good morning to you as well, Munin," Charlotte said. She reached in her pocket and pulled out a small shiny button, holding it up to him.

Munin plucked it from her hand, made a pleased sound, and flew off.

With a slight chuckle, Charlotte started to turn back to the door. Several pumpkins and even some candles had been added around the potted plants, and she remembered that *Samhain* was steadily approaching, marking the end of summer. How could she have forgotten? It was her favorite time of year after all.

Charlotte didn't have long to dwell on the thought before the chimes playfully reached her ears, and she found herself once more at the counter of Brews & Books.

Basil greeted her with his usual smile, although this time it seemed to actually reach his eyes.

Charlotte didn't bother to look at the menu before ordering her usual chai.

"I'll have that to you in just a moment," Basil said as he wrote her alias on a cup and turned away.

While she waited, Charlotte decided to check out a new display of ceramic mugs that had been set up near the counter. Each cup had a unique design as if they'd all been painstakingly made by hand. They ranged from simple and plain to completely ornate. One in particular caught her eye above all others.

The handle had been molded to resemble twisted brown vines, which crept along the cup itself, sprouting tiny vermillion colored buds against a backdrop washed with a deep sparkling blue. It was as if a fall evening had been captured and molded into a lasting memory.

The longer Charlotte looked at the mug, the longer she could have sworn the amber-touched leaves on the vines shifted in a gentle breeze. Stars sparkled in the night sky and pale moonlight illuminated the flower buds. One bud appeared to glow ever so slightly as it began to open.

Charlotte leaned closer to get a better look.

No, don't!

She straightened abruptly with a frown. The mug sat innocently on the display, the vines most definitely not moving. Charlotte shook her head and decided that she really needed to get some decent sleep soon. She couldn't keep imagining things like this.

You cannot always trust your eyes.

"They just arrived this morning," Basil said, suddenly appearing at her side with her order. "Would you like one?"

Charlotte shook her head and told him, "They are quite tempting, but I have too many mugs already." Her eyes drifted back to the vine-covered mug. She really did want it, what would be the harm? It was only one cup, it wouldn't take much room. It took her a moment to realize her hand was a mere breath away from the handle. "Ah." Charlotte withdrew her hand. "No, I have too many, sorry."

"Pity," he said with a gentle smile.

A slight glint on his apron by his nametag caught her attention. Charlotte tilted her head to the side as she found a small button had been sewn there. She could have sworn it hadn't been there before. Wait, wasn't that the button she'd given to Munin? No, it couldn't be, could it? She'd just given it to him outside the shop. There was no way Basil could have it.

"We will have a class tonight on how to make coffee mugs, if you'd like to come," Basil told her.

Charlotte met his eager gaze and offered him a sad smile in return. "It does sound like it would be fun, but unfortunately, I have to work."

He nodded his head, his smile not fading in the least. "Perhaps another time."

Charlotte took her drink and gave her thanks before stepping out the door, Munin following her home.

It was storming terribly when she found herself in front of Brews & Books. Charlotte's heart was racing, but she couldn't remember why. Her breathing was hard, as if she'd run there. What could have been so bad that she ran in such a terrible storm? How could she run to a place that didn't exist? It took Charlotte a moment to realize she was standing in the rain without an umbrella, the rain completely soaking her. She was almost certain she had been crying, but with all the rain, she couldn't tell.

The chimes sounded different today, almost as if they were restless. Could chimes feel restless? No . . . they were chimes. They didn't feel anything. Shaking the thought from her head, Charlotte decided the only thing she really wanted at that moment was to sit down and enjoy something warm to drink. To let her mind wander and not think about everything that troubled her.

As usual, Basil awaited her at the counter with his warm smile. His eyes looked her up and down before he said gently, "Would you like a hot chocolate today? It'll be on the house."

Don't accept gifts.

"That sounds wonderful," Charlotte replied, ignoring the voice for the first time. She was cold and wet, and a warm drink sounded wonderful, especially one that was free.

Basil nodded and grabbed a ceramic coffee mug instead of a togo cup, the same cup with the vine handle that she'd been staring at so intently the day before.

She hadn't said anything about wanting to stay and drink it, yet it was as if he could read her thoughts. Charlotte walked over to one of the tables and ran her fingers along the polished bloodwood before taking a seat for the first time.

No, don't sit. Don't stay.

She shook the thought from her head and rubbed her arms. Really, why had she not brought an umbrella? Had the rain come upon her suddenly? No, she had been running. She was quite certain of that. But running from what? From whom? Charlotte tried to fight the brain fog she felt in the shop, desperately trying to think of who might have been trying to hurt her.

Her thoughts were interrupted as the door to the cafe slammed open, and the chimes sounded distorted, even displeased with this new development. A man stood in the doorway, rain-soaked, his face contorted in anger. Veins bulged on his neck and the side of his forehead.

She remembered why she'd been running now—she'd been running from him. His name was John, and she'd been in a relationship with him, but all he did was lie to her and hurt her. He'd frightened her, and she'd run from him. By the looks of it, he hadn't been all too happy with that.

Their eyes met, and Charlotte's body tensed in response as the urge to run filled her. Her body, however, wouldn't move. She felt as if she was rooted in her chair, her heart racing painfully in her chest. She didn't want the confrontation she knew would happen.

He stomped his way toward her, and suddenly Basil stood between them. Charlotte didn't know when he'd approached, but she was almost certain he hadn't been there a moment ago. He set a steaming cup down gently in front of her before he turned his smile on John.

Charlotte looked up at Basil. His smile was different. There was something new to it. Something dangerous.

"Do you need help?" Basil asked her.

She wanted to say yes, but she hesitated. Would he help her? Would he be able to stop John? Would it be so bad to accept his help?

Be careful.

Charlotte didn't care what the voice said anymore. John had found her, and she wanted to be free of him. Once she decided, she met Basil's eyes firmly and nodded.

"Will you give me your life?"

Don't answer ... don't do it ...

"Yes," Charlotte said without hesitation.

Basil smiled as he turned back to John. "You seem to be a bit upset," he said in a calm tone. "May I have some of your time?"

John scoffed at the question and tried to shove Basil aside. The baristo, however, didn't budge in the slightest. This frustrated John more. "Listen, I'm here to talk to Charlotte, not you."

"Ah, but Charlotte is a valued customer," Basil replied in an even, firm tone. "I'll ask again. May I have some of your time? You're perfectly free to talk to her after."

"Fine, whatever," John replied.

There was a flaw in his choice of words. John didn't know what Charlotte knew. He didn't know who, or what, he was dealing with, and his agreement would be his own downfall.

Basil's smile changed. It no longer was a sweet twist of the lips but a maliciously wide grin with the glint of sharp teeth. Charlotte watched as his form seemed to shift, stretching a bit taller. His eyes darkened, and the floor beneath her feet shuddered.

Charlotte looked down to watch as a dark circle formed beneath Basil and John's feet. She frowned as her eyes were certain the wood floor had turned into a forest floor ringed in mushrooms, but logic told her that was impossible. The normally ethereal music shifted and gained new eerie notes, turning into something more sinister. The lights flickered like an old bulb dying, the darkness moving closer and closer.

A guttural sound emerged from John, drawing her attention. She looked back at him and watched as he seemed to age before her eyes. His cheeks became sunken and his eyes glazed over. His dark hair quickly took on heavy amounts of gray and white while his body thinned dramatically and hunched over.

And then it was over. As quickly as it had started, it was done.

The mushroom ring vanished and the floor was once again wood. The music sweetly played in the background, and the lights warmly illuminated the shop.

John was no longer the young man he once was. All that remained was a broken and shaken old man who struggled to stand upright. He looked around the cafe in confusion. "Where am I?"

"You are in a coffee shop, sir," Basil said in a surprisingly sweet tone.

"Nonsense," John muttered in turn, his body trembling as he

moved. "I don't even like coffee. Why am I here?"

"I believe you came to speak to her." Basil gestured to Charlotte.

She flinched unconsciously when John's hollow gaze met her own.

He shuffled a bit closer, his eyes narrowing as if he tried to see her more clearly. "I don't know her." John grumbled and shuffled his way toward the door. "Eh, you young people and your dang fancy coffee shops."

Charlotte watched as he left, and a wave of relief washed through her. She was finally free of him. Free of John's constant lies and cruel words. Free of his broken promises. Free of...her thoughts trailed off as she glanced back at Basil. Was she really free? She'd just accepted his offer, to give her life.

Basil reached a hand down to trail his finger under her chin. "He will trouble you no more, my dear Charlotte."

Fae don't often get attached, but when they do they can be quite dangerous.

Time seemed to flow differently in Brews & Books, although that didn't seem to bother Charlotte in the least. She watched as seasons came and went. Watched as people walked by the cafe without even noticing its presence. But that was to be expected, as Basil told her. It wasn't easily found by humans. And, unlike her, after the humans had gotten what they wanted, they left the shop never to find it again.

Charlotte was happy there, working the cafe beside Basil. She never felt afraid or worried anymore, never had to face lie after lie from those she thought she loved.

What about your family?

Her hands paused on the cup she was washing. What family? Charlotte thought. She didn't have any family, did she? No, she had no parents or siblings. She'd been all alone, until she'd met John. And now John was no longer a bother to her, and she was happily running the cafe beside Basil.

That's a lie. You had a family.

A face flashed in Charlotte's mind, that of an older woman with threads of gray in her hair. She had a motherly look about her. Could she have been Charlotte's mother? As quickly as the face had come, it was replaced with another, that of a girl who looked a bit younger than Charlotte herself. A sister, perhaps? Another face flashed in her mind of a boy who resembled the girl very much. Oh, and a brother?

Do not lie to yourself. You have a family and a home.

Charlotte shook her head, and she rinsed the mug off before setting it aside to dry. No, she did not know those faces. The only family she had anymore was Basil, and her home was with him above the shop. She was safe and happy there. Nothing else mattered to her. There were no lies with Basil. There was no sadness or fear, only happiness to which she'd never quite felt before.

It's not too late. You can still escape.

She pushed the voice away and focused on the ethereal music that filled the shop, humming as she washed the rest of the cups. What was there to escape from? No, she was perfectly content right where she was.

The gentle chime of the door reached her ears. Charlotte dried her hands on her apron and turned to join Basil at the counter with a warm smile on her lips. Brews & Books had their first visitor of the day.

Leashes

Kiana Lin

I keep my demons on leashes,
They look quiet and polite.
At home they bark and howl and snarl
But, somehow, do not bite.
I feed them when I must—
A little less each day.
I lure them deep into their crates,
Shut them tight, and pray.
Biding time, they lie in wait,
The night belongs to me.
I gather my thoughts in suspect stillness,
They seem to let me be.
But when the morning comes again,
The claw already reaches.
I open up the door, and then—
I walk my demons on leashes.

Lady of Darkness
Lisa Walton

Tuesday

"Mama! Mama! Mamaaaaaaa!"

Her shriek pierces my dreams, jolting me awake. I toss off the covers, my heart hammering in my chest. As I slip from the bed, I glance quickly at Colin. He's lying on his back, mouth hanging open, snoring like a freight train.

How does he not hear her screaming? How does he never hear her screaming?

"Mama! Mamaaaa! Mamaaaaaaaaaaa!"

I race down the hall, hoping to reach her before she wakes the baby.

"Mama, Mamaaa, Mamaaaaaaaaaaaaaaaaaaa!"

"It's okay, Ellie. Mommy's coming. I'll be right there." I push open the door and reach for the lights. "I'm here, Ellie, it's . . ." My voice trails off.

The night terrors have been occurring for over a year. At first, they were random. Then, a few times a week. And, recently, they've been occurring every night.

Every single night, Ellie's scream pulls me from my bed. I run to her and flip on the light. She's cowering in her bed, clenching the covers. Her little fists are white–whether from fear or clasping the blankets so tightly I don't know. Always the same.

Until now.

When I push open the door, the room is already bright. Ellie's bedside lamp is on, and so are the overhead light and her closet light. Her bedding is scattered across the room. The contents of her nightstand drawers are emptied onto the floor. And her closet looks like it's been ransacked by a burglar.

"Ellie, honey, what are you doing?" I struggle to keep my voice calm. My stomach is twisting in knots.

"Mama," she looks at me with frightened eyes. "Where is it? Where did it go?"

I shake my head, confused. "Where is what, Ellie? What are you looking for?"

"My picture," she whispers. "I left it right here before bed."

My panic turns to fury. I haven't slept through the night in over a year, and she's hysterical over a missing picture? At two forty-nine in the morning?

I take a couple of deep breaths and swallow my anger. Even though I don't understand why, I can see she's distraught. Getting mad won't do any good. I brush my hair out of my face and softly pad across the room. I wrap my arms around her.

"It's okay, honey," I say. "I'm sure it's here somewhere. We can find it in the morning."

Panic spreads across her face. "No! I need to find it now." She pulls away and begins frantically rummaging through the things on her floor.

I take a deep breath, hold it for a count of five and let it out. "What picture Ellie? What picture is missing?"

She looks at me. Her warm brown eyes turn dark, inky black, and she sets her thin lips into a hard line.

"It. Was. Right. Here." Ellie points at her nightstand. "I put it right here before bed."

I feel a chill run up my spine. I know the picture she's talking about. Not only that, I took it. I am responsible for this middle-of-the-night rage.

I saw the drawing when I kissed her goodnight. The lights were off, which was a recent development. She'd been sleeping with them on since the night terrors began. But about a week ago, she said, "I'm brave now, Mommy. I'm a big girl. And big girls are brave."

It broke my heart because her little lips quaked when she said it. But she stuck to her word and had been sleeping with the lights off ever since.

But tonight, there was plenty of moonlight spilling through the windows for me to see that drawing sitting on her nightstand.

Ellie loves to draw. She's always carrying around a sketchbook and crayons, and her artwork decorates the house. I could kiss her goodnight one hundred times and not even notice a drawing beside her.

But something about this particular picture caught my eye. And when I looked more closely, I gasped and almost dropped the paper. The drawing showed a little girl with a long braid, presumably Ellie, putting a baby, Malie perhaps, into a box that looked suspiciously like a coffin. There were two more boxes behind her. Next to the girl was a woman drawn all in black, except for her eyes, which were big red circles, her mouth, which was red with pointy black teeth, and the spot where her heart would be, which was covered in a giant red X. The woman was smiling and reaching out her hand toward the little girl.

To say it gave me the creeps is an understatement. That picture made my hands tremble and my stomach lurch.

I looked down at my beautiful sleeping child, long blond hair fanning out around her angelic face. Had she really drawn this picture?

I folded the paper in half and then in half again and slipped it into my pocket. I checked on Malie and then washed my face and brushed my teeth. I put on a pair of sweatpants and an old Def Leppard t-shirt. As I folded my jeans over the chair, I felt the picture in the pocket.

I unfolded it and felt terror coursing through my veins. It was just as creepy as I remembered. I was not sleeping with that drawing in my room.

I slid my feet into a pair of slippers and went downstairs. On the way to the kitchen, I peeked into Colin's office and saw him settling back in his gaming chair, headset firmly in place, shooting at imaginary bogeymen.

Typical.

I lit the burner on the stove, and the corner of the drawing caught fire. I watched as flames danced across the page and dropped it right before they reached my fingertips. Then, I turned off the gas and blew the ashes toward the stove's center. I'd clean them up in the morning.

I certainly can't tell Ellie any of this while she's hysterical, so I soothe and shush and help her search for it. After about twenty minutes, my eyes start drooping, and I feel sick from exhaustion.

"Ellie, come here." I open my arms to her.

Reluctantly, she shuffles over and lets me wrap her up in a hug.

"It's okay," I whisper into her hair, sniffing the sweet smell of lavender shampoo. "We can look more in the morning. I'm sure it will turn up."

"Okay," she whimpers. "I just hope she doesn't get angry."

"Who? Who doesn't get angry."

She pulls away so she can look me in the eye. Then she shakes her head and looks down at her feet.

I bite my lip, not sure whether to press the issue or not. "Ellie, who are you talking about? No one is going to get angry over a picture. Especially not in the middle of the night."

"But that's when she visits me, Mommy. In the middle of the night."

"Oh, sweetie," I say. "Those are just the night terrors. Come on. Let's fix your bed," I replace the sheets and straighten her blankets. Then I climb into her bed, grateful that we got her a queen, and beckon her in beside me. She climbs up and snuggles in, hiding her face on my shoulder.

"I'll be right here. I promise. All night long."

I'm relieved when she falls back to sleep.

In the morning, I'm in the kitchen drinking coffee. Strong coffee. Malie woke up around five fifteen, and I've been up since. She's in her high chair, happily eating Cheerios, so I decide to make Ellie's favorite banana pancakes. Maybe some sprinkles and whipped cream will cheer her up.

Only after I turn on the gas do I remember the picture. I still need to clean up the ashes, and I don't want them to catch on fire. I quickly turn the knob and use a potholder to lift the grate.

But the cooktop is clean. There are no ashes to be found.

Did I clean it up last night? I don't remember doing that. Did Colin clean up the mess? No. I quickly dismiss that thought. He'd never have even noticed ashes on the stove. I shake my head and turn the burner back on.

Ellie is quiet when she comes downstairs, and even the pancakes can't bring a smile to her face. "Did you find it, Mommy?"

"Find what, love?"

She sighs, exasperated. "My picture. The one from my nightstand."

I play dumb. "I'm not sure which one you mean, Ellie. Can you tell me about it?"

"You saw it. When you kissed me goodnight. It was right there on the nightstand. You must have seen it."

I shake my head. "It was dark, Ellie. I didn't see any pictures."

"Yes, you did! I know you did! You probably took it, too! That's what she said!"

I stop flipping pancakes and stare at her. "Who said?" I ask evenly.

Ellie humphs and stamps her foot.

"Ellie, please sit down and eat your pancakes. I put sprinkles on them . . ."

"I don't want any stupid pancakes!" she screams, throwing her plate onto the floor with a crash. Malie starts crying.

"Now look what you've done," I snap, hoisting Malie out of her high chair. I grab a bottle from the fridge and pop it in the bottle warmer.

"Where is it? What did you do with it? What did you do with my drawing? It wasn't yours!" Her voice is shrill, and she's starting to hyperventilate.

Before I can stop myself, I hear the words spilling from my mouth, "Now just calm down, Ellie. You need to get control of yourself and stop screaming at me!" At least I notice the irony.

"You need to stop touching my stuff!" she fires back.

At that moment, Colin comes downstairs. He glares at me and says, "I have a headache, and I'm late. Nobody wants to wake up to this fighting. You girls need to get this sorted out." Then he picks up my coffee cup, drinks it down in one gulp, grabs his backpack, and walks out the door.

"Ugh!" I yell. I pick up the now empty cup and hurl it at the door. Of course, it makes a massive thud as it hits the wood and shatters into a million pieces. The noise sends Malie into another fit of tears.

I feel tears of my own stinging my eyes, and I struggle to hold them back. "I'm sorry, baby girl," I whisper to Malie, rubbing her back. "I'm so sorry. Mommy shouldn't have done that. I shouldn't have lost my temper."

I grab her bottle from the bottle warmer, and she hungrily slurps on it. I survey the kitchen. What a mess.

"Ellie? Ellie, where are you? It's almost time for the bus."

I can't see her in the family room or the dining room.

"Ellie? Ellie, where are you?" I need to find her.

"I'm here, Mommy." Her voice is light. And, dare I say, happy?

She skips into the kitchen, holding a piece of paper. "I found it!"

"You found it?" I echo. "The picture?" No. She could not

possibly mean the picture.

"Yes! It was in Daddy's office."

That was impossible. I burned it to ashes last night. There's no way it would have been in Colin's office.

But the ashes. Where were the ashes?

"Can I see it?" I ask. I need to reassure myself that it is not the same picture.

"No, Mommy. I told you. This picture isn't for you. It's for the lady."

"What lady, Ellie?"

"The lady at the window." Her face falls. "Oops." She puts a hand over her mouth.

"What is it, Ellie?"

"I wasn't supposed to tell you about her. Not yet. I promised. She said you'd make her go away."

Just then, "Viva La Vida" starts playing on my phone. "Time for the bus," I say, relieved to have a reprieve from the conversation.

"Okay." Ellie holds the picture to her chest and then carefully tucks it into her book bag.

I raise my eyebrows. "Hey Ellie, I don't think it's a good idea to take that picture to school."

"Well, I can't leave it here," she says, looking at me defiantly.

The bus honks. "Fine. But do not show that picture to anyone at school."

"Of course not, silly," she says. "Why would I do that?"

I watch Ellie get on the school bus, settle Malie in for her nap, and call the pediatrician. I'm concerned about these visions of the lady in the window. This has never been a part of the night terror before. The phone rings and rings, and I leave a message.

After cleaning up the mess in the kitchen, I turn the coffee pot on to brew another pot and lie down on the couch for a minute. I'm so tired. I haven't gotten a full night's sleep since Malie was born. Often, I'm up two and three times per night. Nothing can prepare you for the total body exhaustion of going more than a year without sleep.

But today feels different. The last few days have felt different. My limbs are heavy, and my brain is operating in slow motion. I hope I'm not getting sick.

The familiar ringtone of my phone permeates my sleep. I rub my eyes and reach for my phone. "Hello?"

"Mrs. Barrington?"

"Yes."

"This is Ramira from Dr. Stein's office. I'm returning your call."

I sit up straighter, anxious to talk to someone about Ellie's visions. "Yes, thank you. It's my daughter Ellie. She's still waking in the night with the night terrors. And just recently . . ."

"Yes?" she prods.

"Well, the thing is, she says that a woman visits her room each night." Saying it out loud sounds ridiculous. "Obviously, this isn't happening," I hurry to explain. "But, it's quite disturbing, and I was, uh, just wondering if this was . . . um, normal. With the night terrors?"

"Well," she begins slowly, "hallucinations are not unusual with night terrors."

"Oh, good . . . "

"But," she continues, "Dr. Stein was hoping Ellie's night terrors would have ended by now. It says here that they started about fifteen months ago?"

"Yes, that's about right. Shortly after her baby sister was born."

"Ah . . . Well, adding a new baby to the family can be a stressful time for a child. How do Malie and Ellie get on now?"

"They adore each other."

"Have Ellie's terrors shown any sign of improvement?"

I let out a long breath. "No. I'd say they are getting worse."

I hear her speaking in a muffled voice to someone in the office. She clears her throat and says, "Mrs. Barrington, Dr. Stein would like to refer you to a child psychiatrist. We've already ruled out any physical reasons for Ellie's night terrors. Maybe a psychiatrist can help you get to the bottom of these or at least provide Ellie with some coping mechanisms to manage them."

This is what I had wanted all along. All those months ago, I requested a referral. But Dr. Stein assured me night terrors were perfectly normal, and most kids outgrow them quickly.

I had researched night terrors on my own. I read every article and book I could get my hands on. And I'm just not convinced that's what is going on with Ellie.

At her next check-up, I brought up my concerns, but Dr. Stein said to give it a few more months. Most kids grow out of them by age six, he assured me. Going to school will make her tired, and she'll sleep better at night.

So much for that.

I take down the information and call the psychiatrist. The first available appointment is a week from Thursday.

That taken care of, I go into the kitchen to pour a cup of coffee. I'm surprised the coffee machine is off. Didn't I brew a second pot? I look at the carafe and see it's full. But when I pour a cup, it isn't steaming like I expected.

I glance at the clock on the microwave. No. That can't be right. Twelve twenty-one? Had I really been asleep for three hours?

That means that Malie has been asleep for three hours, too? She hasn't taken a nap that long since she was an infant. I feel a terror creep into my chest. What if she's sick? Or . . .

Abandoning my lukewarm coffee, I take the stairs two at a time. I sprint down the hallway towards Malie's room.

I push open the door and gasp.

Malie is sitting happily in her crib, nibbling on a crayon and stroking a dolly's hair. Crayons aren't toxic, are they? No, they couldn't be. But where had she gotten a crayon from?

"Hi, sweet baby girl."

"Mama," she says, reaching out her arms.

Has she just been sitting here this whole time? That's not like Malie. When I pick her up, I get a good look at the doll she's holding. It's one of those old-fashioned rag dolls with yarn for hair. I've never seen it before. And I'm sure it was not in Malie's crib when I put her down earlier.

"What's this?" I asked, reaching for the dolly.

She pulls it to her, tightening her fingers around the neck. "Mine!" she screeches.

Okay. I let go. I'll have to ask Ellie about it later. I reach in the crib to grab her blankie and feel something hard. I push the other blankets aside and freeze. Ellie's sketchbook is in the crib. And the book is open to a drawing just as frightening as the one I saw last night.

Maybe more so.

The evil lady, that's how I've come to think of her, is holding a small child out a window and grinning maniacally, showing all her pointy teeth. At the bottom of the page is a small pool filled with spiky rocks. Another twisted body, with a long braid, is lying on top of them.

I pull Malie closer to me, glad she doesn't understand the horror of this picture. Then, I tuck the notebook under my arm, and we go downstairs.

While Malie eats lunch, I flip through the sketchbook. Each page features the evil lady in a variety of menacing positions. Holding a knife over a sleeping child, setting a house on fire, tying a noose on a beam. How on earth does Ellie know what a noose looks like?

Most of the pictures feature water. Children at the bottom of a swimming pool, a lake, a river, or submerged in the bathtub. My instinct is to burn the whole book. Although, after this morning, I wonder if that would do any good.

I don't want it in our home. But I should save it as evidence for the psychiatrist. Evidence of what, I'm not sure.

After lunch, Malie and I go for a walk. She points to trees and dogs, and when we come home, we run around in the backyard chasing bubbles. I almost forget about the fear holding court in my chest.

When Ellie gets home from school, she's all smiles. "We had a guest reader today. She read us *Dragons Love Tacos*. It was so funny. Then we made tacos. Out of paper. Not the eating kind. And I got all my spelling words right, so guess what? No homework!"

I make some popcorn. She chatters about her day and seems perfectly normal. I can't believe she drew the pictures in that sketchbook. I want to ask her about them. And why she put the sketchbook in Malie's crib. But I'm afraid of upsetting her. Or, maybe, I'm just afraid of her answers.

Instead, we play Uno and Chutes and Ladders, and I set up the bouncy castle outside. The girls bounce, and Malie squeals in delight every time Ellie does a flip or bounces hard enough to make her fall over.

I do an online search for "scary children's drawing," and I'm blown away by the number of results. The search results don't make me feel better, exactly, but at least I know Ellie is not the only child with a vivid imagination.

I hope that's all this is.

Colin texts to say he'll be late and not to wait on him for dinner. As if he's ever home for dinner. I make the girls chicken nuggets and pour myself a bourbon. Then we watch *Dinosaur Train* and read some stories before bed.

"What's this?" Ellie asks, picking up Malie's ugly doll.

"Mine!" screeches Malie, pulling the doll out of Ellie's hands.

Ellie widens her eyes and looks at me curiously.

I shrug. "I was going to ask you about that. It was in Malie's crib when she woke up from her nap. I've never seen it before."

Ellie's eyes go dark.

"Do you know where it came from?"

She shakes her head and mutters something under her breath.

"What was that?"

"Nothing." But I swear I heard her say, "Oh, no."

Wednesday

I wake up in the middle of the night, disoriented. The first thing I notice is the quiet. No one is calling my name. Or crying. Or screaming. I illuminate my phone to check the time. Two thirty-nine.

There's no use going back to sleep now. Ellie will be calling for me within the hour. I lay in the dark, listening to my husband grunt and snore. I feel disgusted. How have I wound up here? In this house? In this life? With this partner?

I love my girls with all my heart, but this is not the life I planned. I start to go down the rabbit hole of "what ifs."

What if I hadn't gone to Boston that weekend?

What if I hadn't wound up killing time in that dinky little bar?

What if I said no when Colin asked me to dinner?

What if I hadn't given up my job as a security analyst to move here?

What if my parents were still alive?

What if I had gone back to work after Ellie was born?

What if Malie was never born?

What if Colin were ever home?

What if we left him months ago?

I brush the thoughts from my head and check the clock in five-minute increments. I'm shocked it's still quiet.

The next time I wake up, I hear footsteps. I fumble in the dark for my phone, which has gotten lodged under my pillow. Four twenty-one. Almost dawn. And still, no one's crying.

You'd think I'd be relieved. But I'm not. Why haven't my girls called for me? I slip from the bed, throw my robe around my shoulders, and tiptoe down the hall. I peek in on Malie, who is sleeping soundly, clutching her blankie in one hand and that ugly doll in the other.

Then I check on Ellie. As soon as I push open her door, she says, "Sssh! Mommy, come here."

"Ellie, you're awake?" I say in my normal voice.

"Ssshhh!" she says more forcefully. She waves me over to her bed.

I cross the room and sit down beside her. She clasps my hand and strokes my hair. "Do you see her, Mommy?"

I look at my daughter and follow her gaze to the corner of the room near the window. There is nothing to see except a Peppa Pig backpack and a tiara.

"See who, baby?"

"The lady. Look," she points. "She's watching us."

Her words make my heart jump. My neck feels clammy. "There's no one there, sweetie. It's just a shadow." I reach for her bedside lamp.

"Noooo!" Ellie shrieks. But it's too late. My fingers have already turned the switch, and soft light spills into the room. Ellie shakes her head at me. "She doesn't like the light, Mommy. She is a lady of darkness."

The matter-of-factness with which she says this makes my gut twist with dread. I don't sleep the rest of the night. I just lie there holding Ellie tight. Ready to protect her from the lady of the darkness.

Later that morning, I'm packing Ellie's lunch and listening to Malie babble while she plays with her ball popper. Every few seconds, I stop for another swig of coffee, determined to finish the whole pot before Colin comes downstairs.

Spiteful? Maybe. But he deserves it.

He hadn't come home until after ten last night, which was well after the girls were bathed and put to bed. I'd cleaned the house, polished off a second bourbon, and was dozing on the couch while *Chopped* played in the background.

I wanted to show him the sketchbook. Not because I thought he'd help me understand it, but because it's heavy knowledge to carry on my own. I'm sick of doing everything on my own.

But he walked right past me as though he didn't even see me, went into his office, and shut the door. Within minutes, I heard him talking to his gaming friends. Apparently, I'm married to an adolescent boy.

Fury eclipsed my fear, and I went to bed, falling fast asleep.

Ellie comes downstairs and slumps into a chair. She lays her head on the table.

"Ellie, are you okay?"

"Mmmm," she grunts.

"What's wrong?"

"I'm soooo tired," she whines.

I massage my temples. Same, girl. Same. I thought we all slept better last night. But maybe not.

I was up listening for ghosts. And Ellie was wide awake when I went into her room. Who knows how long she'd been awake?

"I'm sorry, baby." I ruffle her hair. "Do you want some toast?"

"No."

"Cereal? I have Rice Krispies or Honey Nut Cheerios."
"No."
"How about some chocolate milk?"
"No."
"Do you want me to braid your hair?"
She sat up straighter. "Yes, please."
Her response surprises me. I grab the brush and start to carefully brush out the tangles.

As I work my fingers through her hair, she says, "Did you really not see her, Mommy? You didn't see the lady in the window?"

My voice catches in my throat. "No, baby, I'm sorry. I didn't see anyone."

"Am I the only one who can see her?" she asks.

"I don't know, honey."

"I know she's there, Mommy. Every night she watches me. She used to just come to the window. But now she comes inside. Sometimes, she rubs my hair like you do or tickles my cheek. But usually, she just watches. She's always watching. She says she's the lady of the darkness."

"What's this? Who's always watching?" asks Colin.

I shoot Ellie a look, even though I know it's not reasonable to expect my six-year-old to interpret secret glances. "The lady in the window," Ellie says. "She comes when I'm sleeping."

Colin stops and stares at Ellie, sizing her up like she's a freak in the circus. "That's enough, Ellie. Enough of this nonsense. Enough of the screaming and crying in the night. Enough of waking up the whole house. And enough of imaginary monsters. It's time to grow up." As if he ever wakes up to help her. "If I hear another word about this, you'll be sorry."

He slams his hand down on the table and storms out the door.

Ellie bursts into tears and flings herself on the floor. Not to be outdone, Malie starts wailing too. I stand in the kitchen watching my two daughters fall apart. My fists are clenched, my body shakes with rage, and I summon the strength to stay calm.

Malie is easy to distract. I give her a banana and a spoon and let her go to town. Ellie is another story.

She talks about how the lady is real, and no one believes her, and Daddy is so mean. I can't disagree with the last point.

And then she says something that makes me freeze. "We don't have much time left, Mommy. It's almost time to go."

I want to believe she's talking about the school bus or

something equally innocuous, but in my bones, I know she is talking about the lady of darkness.

Eventually, long after the bus has come and gone, I manage to console her. I send her upstairs to wash her face and tell her to meet me in the front hall, and we can stop at Starbucks on the way to school. I figure she's already late—what's another fifteen minutes?

To my surprise, this news makes her face light up. When she comes downstairs, she looks so much calmer and ready to face the day. "Can I get a cake pop and a hot chocolate?"

"Sure," I say. "You can have anything you want."

I strap Malie into her car seat and make sure Ellie's seat belt is fastened. But as I check the buckle, I have an eerie feeling that a seatbelt is not nearly enough to keep her, or any of us, safe.

After we drop Ellie off at school, we go to the park for a walk. I need to get out of the house and clear my head. It still feels like I'm walking through a fog. After a brisk walk around the duck pond, I let Malie run around the toddler playground and push her on the swing.

She nods off before we even leave the parking lot. I carry her into the house and up to her crib. As I climb the stairs, I hear a strange sound, a familiar sound. A sound like running water.

The dishwasher? The washing machine? I don't remember turning either of them on, but I've been so tired it's hard to remember anything. I check the appliances, but neither is running.

Still, I hear the whooshing sound of water running through the pipes. I check the powder room downstairs and then head upstairs. Maybe Ellie left the water running when she washed her face.

As I push open the door to the girls' bathroom, my mouth falls open in shock. Water runs over the tub and spills onto the floor. There's already almost an inch of standing water.

"What the . . ." I splash through the puddle and reach to turn the water off. "Ouch!" It's scalding.

I groan with frustration. Part of me just wants to lie down, right here on the bathroom floor. I don't even care about the hot water. But I muster the energy to gather a bunch of old towels and soak up the mess. Tears sting the back of my eyes.

When is it going to get easier?

Had the water been running when we left the house? Had Ellie turned on the tub when she came upstairs to wash her face? Why would she have done that? It's not like her to purposely flood the house. Not one bit. Clearly, she's more troubled than I realized. I'm so glad we have that appointment coming up.

When Ellie gets off the school bus, she's bubbly. "We went on a leaf walk today. Then, we made leaf people from the leaves we collected. And we counted by twos. It's easy. Two, four, six, eight, ten. And then, we drew with chalk on the sidewalk."

This last part gets my attention. I lick my lips. "What did you draw?" I wonder if I want to know the answer.

"Sadie and I drew cupcakes and cookies. We're going to make a bakery."

I exhale and smile. "That sounds fun. Ellie." I hate the thought of ruining her good mood, but I have to ask. "Did you turn on the bathtub when you went upstairs before school?"

She narrows her eyes and wrinkles her brow. "What?" she snaps. "No. Why would I do that?"

"I don't know, honey. But when Malie and I got home, the tub was running. The water had overflowed and spilled all over the floor. It was a giant mess."

Ellie's face turns white, and her mouth opens into an O. She shakes her head and says, "I have to go upstairs." She races up the stairs before I can stop her.

Malie totters over to the stairs and says, "E-ye? E-ye?"

I smile down at her. "Ellie is tired," I say. Although I have no idea why she went upstairs in such a hurry.

"Nigh, nigh." Malie waves to the stairs.

I scoop her up and twirl her around. "Come on, sweetie, let's play blocks."

Malie and I sit on the floor. I build a tower, and she knocks it down. Over and over and over again.

About an hour later, Ellie comes downstairs. "Have you seen my sketchbook?" she asks.

I look up and bite my lip. "No. Have you looked in your room?"

She huffs at me. Is she six or sixteen? "Obviously."

I ignore her tone. "How about Malie's room?"

She wrinkles her nose. "Why would it be in there?"

Unless she is a fantastic actress, she did not put her sketchbook in Malie's crib.

I shrug. "Well, didn't you find your picture in Dad's office? Maybe it's in there."

She sighs and heads off to the office.

"More!" demands Malie, and I stack the blocks again.

Ellie returns to the living room with a glass of water. She

slides down to the floor with us and starts stacking blocks.

"Did you find it?"

"No." She sounds dejected. "It's not there."

"Don't you have another sketchbook?"

She sighed. "Yeah, but we're going to have to start over."

I raise my eyebrows, but she doesn't elaborate.

"Let's build a city," I suggest. We build silently for the next few minutes, but looking at Ellie, she's deep in thought just as I am. Even the baby looks like she's concentrating.

"Baaaa!" says Malie as she smashes the city. I laugh, and Ellie takes a big sip of her water.

"Yuck! What's wrong with this water?" She coughs and spits it out.

"Where did you get that?" I ask.

"It was in the office. I left it there this morning."

I think back to this morning. I remember the meltdown. The crying. The screaming. I do not remember her getting a glass of water. "Are you sure?"

"Yeah, but this is yucky." She hands me the glass.

I sniff and shudder. "Ellie, this isn't water. It's vodka."

"Vodka?"

"Yes. Alcohol. Not for little girls. Can you show me where you got it?"

She nods and jumps up. It takes me a little longer to get to my feet, and then I grab Malie's hand. "Come on."

We march to the office, which is a pigsty. It smells like stale cigarettes—was Colin really smoking in the house with two small children?

"It was right here. Where I left it." She points to a side table next to the couch. All the way across the room from Colin's gaming station. It seems like an unlikely place for him to leave a drink. And he usually drinks beer or Scotch.

But how would Ellie have gotten vodka? It must have been Colin. I can't believe he left it here for her to find.

Colin doesn't come home until well after eleven o'clock. I don't wait up for him. I put the girls to bed and spend an extra half hour with Ellie reading *Judy Moody*.

When I leave her room, she says, "Mommy, please leave the light on."

"I thought you were a big girl now." Immediately, I regret my choice of words.

"I am. I'll turn it off in a bit. That's the way she likes it. But I need to finish my drawing first."

I inhale sharply and swallow back a thousand objections. Instead, I simply nod. "Okay, don't stay up too late."

I check on her before I go to bed, and she is sleeping on her side. The lamp is still on, and the new sketchbook is open to her latest drawing. A small child and a slightly larger child with a braid stand over a woman lying on the floor. The children are laughing. The lady of darkness lurks on the edge of the page.

My hand reaches out to snatch the page. But I remember Ellie's hysteria from a couple of nights ago, and I draw my hand back. It feels wrong to leave it there while she's sleeping. But what else can I do?

I hear Colin come home. He slams the door behind him and causes a loud commotion when he enters the office. I have no idea where he's been or when he's coming to bed. But the only thing I care about is that he doesn't wake the girls. I hold my breath for what feels like hours.

Thursday

The next time I open my eyes, it's cold in the room. Colin has stolen all the covers and is snoring beside me. I lift my head and listen in the dark. Is Ellie calling for me? Or was it Malie?

No. Oh no! I jump out of bed and run down the hall. It's the damn bathtub running again.

I push open the door to the girls' bathroom. Why was it closed? And dash over to the tub. Luckily, I heard it in time. I turn the tap off and lean over, putting my hands on my knees to catch my breath.

I pull the plug and watch the water swirl down the drain. Then I make my way across the hall to Ellie's room. I hesitantly push open her door, but she is sound asleep. I kiss her forehead, but she doesn't stir.

There's no way she turned on the tub just a few moments ago. Which means . . . I don't want to think about what it means.

I leave her room and head down the hall to check on Malie. She's sleeping peacefully, clutching that stupid doll. I gently feel around her crib but don't feel the sketchbook.

Outside of my bedroom, I pause. I hear Colin snoring from out here. So I go back to Ellie's room and climb in beside her. I put my arm around her, and she snuggles into my neck.

"Mama. Mama. Mama," I hear my name being hissed from far away.

"Mama. Mommy. Mommy, wake up." I open my eyes and see Ellie's face inches from mine. "Mommy," she whispers. "Be very quiet and look at the corner by the window."

I blink and rub my tired eyes. "Okay," I say groggily, trying to focus on my daughter. I look toward the corner. Nothing is there. "Oh," I say.

"Oh?" she echoes.

I can hardly keep my eyes open.

I feel Ellie slapping my face. "Mommy, wake up. Look!" she points again.

I still don't see anything. "I'm sorry, baby, I don't see anything."

"You can't see her?" Her voice is incredulous.

I shake my head. "I believe that you see her. But I can't see her."

She inhales deeply. And then very slowly lets out her breath. She pats my shoulder. "It's okay, Mommy. It doesn't matter anyway. You'll see her soon."

Then she snuggles into my arms and goes back to sleep.

"Kirsten! Kirsten! What the hell are you doing? Get the hell up. It's half past seven. The baby's crying. There's no coffee. And If you don't drag your sorry ass out of bed right now, Ellie's going to miss the bus!" My husband's voice rushes into my mind.

I open my eyes, surprised to see that it's light outside. I rub my temple and blink. It takes all my energy to roll over. I feel like I'm lying in quicksand.

Slowly, I turn to the door, but Colin's already gone. Gently, I shake Ellie. "Good morning, sunshine. It's time to rise and shine." She rolls over and throws an arm over her eyes.

"Okay," she mumbles but puts her head under the pillow.

I climb out of bed and glance at the nightstand. Ellie's drawing is gone. In its place is a large glass of water.

My throat is parched, and I reach for it. Had I brought this glass in last night? Seeing the water makes me think of the bathtub, and I listen carefully. But all is quiet.

I pick up the glass and carry it over to the window. I look outside, but all I see is the giant elm tree. Nothing is out of place in the corner, either. I take a big swig and then spit it right out.

Vodka again! Ugh! I hate vodka!

Who is leaving glasses of vodka around the house? Was this Colin's idea of a sick joke?

On the way to my bedroom, I check the bathroom again. Just to be sure. The tub is dry.

I throw on a sweatshirt and go to Malie's room. She's sitting with her back to me, looking out the window. She's babbling and flailing her hands about like she's having an animated conversation, albeit in baby code. Then she sits quietly, tilting her head. More nonsensical sounds. Followed by silence while she listens.

"Good morning Malie," I say in a sing-song voice. She raises her little hand in the air as if telling me to stop and reaches toward the window. I'm not sure why, but her actions are unsettling, and I rush over to the crib and lift her out.

Malie goes stiff in my arms, and she lets out a sharp screech. I hold her to me. "Malie, it's just Mommy. Good morning, sweetie."

She grabs my hair and coos. "Mama?" Her voice sounds unsure.

"Yes, Mama."

"Mama! Mama!" She snuggles in and pops her thumb in her mouth. That's odd. I've never seen her suck her thumb before. Perhaps the stress is getting to all of us. I just pray that her anxiety doesn't manifest itself in night terrors.

By the time we get downstairs, Colin is gone. Of course, he hasn't bothered to make coffee. Since we're already running late, I tell Ellie I'll drive her to school again.

"Starbucks?" she asks hopefully.

"Sure," I said. I don't have the energy to fight and need some coffee to clear the cobwebs from my head.

It's drizzling, so Malie and I go to the grocery store instead of the park. Malie eats cheese and a chocolate chip cookie. I push her around in a daze.

When we return to the house, I carry Malie inside on one hip and juggle two grocery bags on the other. I set her up watching *Octonauts* and hurry to the car for the rest of the bags. While I'm unpacking them in the kitchen, I notice the familiar whoosh of water through the pipes.

"Damnit!" I yell. Not again. I speed up the stairs and push open the bathroom door just in time to see the water inching to the top of the tub. What the hell is going on?

I turn off the faucet and sit on the edge of the tub, panting. I rub my knuckles into my eyes, trying to think. I play with the knobs.

They don't feel loose to me. The only explanation is that someone is turning on the tap. Nothing else makes sense.

But who? There's no one here.

Was it Colin? Had he come home while we were out? Is he trying to make me think I was going crazy?

Am I going crazy? Maybe it isn't Ellie who needs to see the psychiatrist. Maybe it's me.

"No, no, no . . ." I shake my head. I look at the knobs, like they can explain what's going on.

Again, I take to searching the internet for "tub turns on by itself." The first three pages of results are about jacuzzi tubs whose jets turn on by themselves. Usually, a faulty electrical system is to blame. That makes sense. But there isn't anything about defective plumbing systems.

I keep scrolling, hoping to find something, anything to convince me I'm not going crazy.

And there, on the fourth page, I see something that catches my eye. It's a news article from 1984. "Woman Says New House Is Haunted: Tub Turns On; Overflows."

I click the link and skim the article, which is a blurry PDF of a newspaper clipping. According to the article, a family moved into a new house and started noticing odd happenings. Things would mysteriously disappear only to turn up later in plain sight. The windows would open and close on their own. And the tub would run by itself. The woman interviewed for the article said she never saw a ghost but felt an evil presence, and she quickly moved her family to her sister's place and sold the house.

Hmmm . . . I wonder . . .

No, this article says Magnolia Springs, AL. That's a long way from here.

But an idea starts to form.

I type "haunted house" and "Brookshire Drive, Hillford" into the search bar but then think better of it. I'm not going down that road. I slide the phone into my pocket and head back downstairs.

In the afternoon, Malie and I play with her little animals. She's still clutching that ugly doll. I wish I knew where it came from. The rain is pelting the roof with a steady *rap, rap, rap,* and the wind is howling. From where I sit on the floor, I can see the tops of the trees bending in the gusts. It almost feels like a hurricane.

Then something catches my eye. A shadow? It's fuzzy through the window and the rain, but it looks like a person at the door. I wait for the knock.

Instead, a loud crash of thunder causes us both to jump, and Malie shrieks. "It's okay, baby," I say, picking her up. The next bolt of lightning pitches the room into darkness.

"Ooooh," she cries in surprise.

"Let's find some candles."

I carry her into the dining room and set her beside me as I squat down to hunt through the buffet. I find a tarnished silver tea set, some holiday platters adorned with dancing penguins, a stack of mismatched paper napkins, a couple old bottles of wine and one of sherry, and two boxes of plastic silverware. But no candles.

"Come on," I say, "let's check the pantry." She toddles after me to the kitchen and runs her hand along the air vent as I hunt for candles. I turn on the flashlight on my phone and dig around the bottom shelf behind the picnic basket, cooler bags, and about thirty plastic water bottles.

"Yes!" I say and raise two pillar candles triumphantly. I sniff. Pine and peppermint. Oh well, they will have to do. I turn to show the candles to Malie, but she's gone.

"Malie?" My pulse quickens, and I rush back to the family room. I smile when I see she's playing with her little animals. "Mommy found the candles." She doesn't acknowledge me.

I light them and join her on the floor. "The duck says quack," I say, doing my best imitation of quacking.

Malie laughs. She loves the duck noise. But then her face grows serious, and she points over to the foyer to the left of the stairs. I follow her chubby little finger with my eyes, but I don't see anything unusual.

"What's over there, baby? What do you see?"

She doesn't answer me, of course. But she pushes herself up, and her eyes dart back and forth between me and the wall beside the stairs.

Please don't go over there.

She bobbles over to her book basket and takes out a board book about colors. I smile. Nothing to worry about.

Until, with the book in hand, Malie makes her way to the stairs and plops herself down inches from the wall. She opens the book, and points to pictures, babbling away. Then she blows a kiss in the direction of the wall.

I watch silently, terror rising in the pit of stomach. Just like in her crib earlier, it looks like she is reading with someone. Someone I can't see. Someone in the wall.

"Malie," I say. "Let's go get some lunch." I'm not hungry, but I need to distract her.

"K," she says. Then, turning to look back at the stairs one more time, she waves. "Bye."

By the time Ellie gets home, my nerves are frayed. I never quite cleared the morning fogginess from my brain, and between the unexplained running bathtub and Malie's strange behavior, not to mention all those pictures in the sketchbook I see every time I close my eyes, I am starting to lose it.

The rain is still falling outside, but luckily the power came back on as we ate lunch. I suggest we snuggle and watch *Sing*. The girls get comfortable in my arms, and it's not long before they're sound asleep. I close my eyes, too.

When I open them, the movie has ended. Both girls are still cuddled up on the couch—Ellie in a little ball with her head on the pillow and Malie lying across my lap. Gently, I move her to the cushion and get up.

I'm about to head to the kitchen when I notice a tall glass of water on the coffee table. And a page from the sketchbook.

I don't want to look. But I have to. I peer down at the drawing.

This picture shows two children lying in the bottom of a bathtub. Water flows over the top of the tub and onto the floor. A woman is lying on the floor, the water only inches from her head. And in the upper corner, the evil lady is grinning.

I rub my eyes, hoping it's just an illusion. But when I look again, the drawing is still there. Carefully, I reach out my fingers and touch the paper. It's real.

Then I lift the glass and sniff. Vodka. I sink down to my knees and cover my face with my hands. I choke back the sobs so as not to wake the girls. My whole body is shaking.

This can't be happening.

After some time, I have no idea how long I've been sitting like that. I shift my weight and stretch out my legs. My foot kicks something under the table. I reach down to retrieve what I expect to be an animal or maybe a block. My hand closes around a small glass jar.

How strange.

The bottle is clear glass and about three inches tall. There are five red and blue pills inside. A faded label reads Iwnal? Twnal? Tumal? I can't tell.

I Google "Tumal." The results page takes me to Tuinal, a

sleeping pill popular in the 1940s. How did this old pill bottle wind up in my family room?

I look at the pills. Is someone drugging me? Is that why I always feel so foggy? Someone would have to be Colin.

But honestly, we don't spend enough time together for him to pull off something like that.

I make my way into the kitchen and pour a real glass of water from the fridge. I down it in one gulp and refill the glass.

Then I walk back through to the family room. I smile at the girls sleeping on the couch. Then I hear it. The now familiar rush of water as the bathtub fills. We're the only ones here, the girls and me. And none of us has turned on the tub.

There's only one explanation. And I no longer need Google to help me understand. I think back to the article I read about the haunted house.

That's when I see her, materializing in front of the window, near the stairs. I'm not even surprised. The drawings aren't an exact likeness but close enough.

"It's time," she says. "Get the girls. Ellie first. She's ready."

I know what I'm supposed to do. There's really no other choice. It's what I've always been supposed to do. I just didn't see it.

I take in a big breath, then go to the couch. I shake Ellie gently to wake her and whisper in her ear.

Ellie looks from me to the lady and grimaces. She grabs my hand and squeezes.

I hope she can read my eyes this time. The lady watches us the entire time.

"Ellie," she says.

Ellie shakes her head and clutches my hand. I rub my thumb on her fingers and heave Malie to my hip. She starts to whine.

"Sssh, baby. It will be okay."

"Ready?" asks the lady of the darkness.

"Can you check the water first, please? It's been so hot."

"Of course," she says. "You're a good mom. Just like me." She ascends the stairs.

As soon as she disappears from view, I dash for the front door, grabbing my purse from the hook and dragging Ellie behind me. I'm breathing hard and both girls are crying. But I pull the door shut behind us and we spill down the stairs. I buckle Malie into her carseat. My hands shake so badly it takes three tries.

I put the car in gear and peel out of the driveway before the lady of darkness can appear. I expect her to try and stop us, but, miraculously, she does not follow.

Later that night, when we are settled in a hotel room and the girls are sleeping, I finally push enter on the search "haunted house, Brookshire Drive, Hillford." The first page is flooded with results.

Neighbors say house is haunted after double murder-suicide

Woman murders daughters; kills self.

Woman drowns babies in bathtub.

Is Lara's ghost still here?

I click on the first article.

October 29, 1979. HILLFORD - Cecil County police were called to 13 Brookshire Drive on October 27 to investigate a trespasser and discovered massive water damage in the kitchen. Officers speculate a pipe must have burst.

The house has been vacant since 1974, after the previous residents, Janelle and Melvin Shay, moved out unexpectedly in the middle of the night. In 1977, the County repossessed the house for nonpayment of taxes, and it was sold at auction to anonymous buyers. But said buyers never moved into the house.

Instead, they listed it with Hawthorn Realty. Madison Hawthorn says, "I really hope the police get to the bottom of this. The buyers have spent a ton of money fixing up this place. It's the perfect home for a young family. I've shown that house dozens of times and never witnessed anything strange. And this is no burst pipe. I had my inspector out here today, and he said the plumbing is fine. I blame the damage on a prankster."

Neighbor Leslie Waterman disagrees. "This is not the work of a prankster. This is Lara. Lara Sketchins. She still haunts the place. We see her in the windows and on the porch. And sometimes, we can even hear her crying. She's responsible for that mess in the kitchen. I just know it."

In 1941, Lara Sketchins killed her two young daughters, June, 6, and Emily, 1, before killing herself.

The children were found submerged in the bathtub. Lara was discovered dead in her bed. She died from a lethal combination of Tuinal and vodka.

A photo accompanies the article. The older girl, June, had a long brown braid. And the baby, Emily, was sucking her thumb and clutching a doll that looked suspiciously like the ugly doll Malie has become attached to.

I tremble.

I wish I had researched this sooner. But no one wants to think their house is haunted. I look at my sleeping daughters and feel immense relief that we escaped.

Friday

I wake feeling rested. For the first time in months, I slept all night, and my brain doesn't feel cloudy.

The girls are still sleeping, and the ugly doll has been discarded on the floor. I scoop up the hideous toy and toss her in the wastebasket. Then, I take the trash bag out, tie it up, and place it outside of the room.

"Mommy?" says Ellie.

"Good morning, Ellie."

"Are we going to stay here?"

"For a couple of days."

I haven't thought through the logistics of what's next for us. All I know is we will never return to the house. And I'm not going back to Colin.

I do have to let him know we're safe. But I checked my phone last night and again this morning, and he hasn't called or texted me yet. Maybe he doesn't even know we're missing.

"And then we're going home?"

"No, love. I'm sorry. We can't go back there."

She smiles. "Good. I didn't like that lady." She's quiet for a minute and says, "Can we get pancakes?"

"Sure, when Malie wakes up."

"And can I get a new sketchbook?"

"Okay," I say with only minor trepidation.

I grab the carafe from the mini coffee maker and make a pot of coffee. When I look back at the girls, Ellie is drawing on the tiny hotel notepad. I smile, not surprised she couldn't wait for a new sketchbook. I hope she's drawing unicorns and rainbows.

Then, I go into the bathroom to brush my teeth. In the mirror, I catch the reflection of the bathtub. I freeze. Slowly, I turn around.

No.

It's not possible.

The bathtub is full. Sitting on the side of the tub is a plastic glass full of clear liquid.

About the Fireside Authors
(In order of appearance)

B. K. CLARK is a homeschooling mother of four boys who subsists solely on caffeine and words. Although she got her start writing poetry, she focuses mostly on fiction with deep, emotional storylines and lives to make you "feel" while reading her work.

TRISTAN TUTTLE is a writer and poet who lives in north Georgia with her husband, Jared, and their two daughters, Jubilee and Rejoice. She spends her days chasing her girls through the garden rows and writing about it. Her debut poetry collection *A Kudzu Vine of Blood and Bone* was a #1 New Release on Amazon. She can be found at tristantuttle.com as well as on Instagram @tristantuttle and Facebook @tristantuttlewrites.

BRITTA BROWN is the very tired mother of two boys under five, an energetic lab-mix, and several dozen misbehaving witches, elves, vampires, and fantastical creatures that live in her head. When not busy wrangling her children (both real and fictional), she can be found running the many cul-de-sacs of her neighborhood or researching fusion taco recipes. She is an avid reader of romantic fantasy and studied Comparative Literature and UC Irvine, combining the knowledge of both to poke loving fun at the rest.

JENNIFER DOVE LEWIS is an emerging women's fiction author, who also likes to dabble around in young adult fiction and horror. She lives in sunny Tucson, AZ with her family and their many furry (and some scaly!) pets. Her biggest passion is putting words on paper, but she also loves baking, gardening, reading, and binge-watching her favorite TV shows.

ANNA MINOR-WEEKS was raised down the street from an enchanted forest, breathing in magic and breathing out wonder. Even though she never received her Hogwarts letter and never found a portal to Wonderland, Neverland, or Narnia, Anna had a delightful childhood surrounded by her loving family. With a dusty degree in English literature from Saint Martin's University and a graveyard of stories, Moms Who Write has inspired her to keep pursuing her dream of being an actual writer. Anna lives nestled in the beautiful Pacific Northwest with her devoted husband and her three wonderful children (one who is in-utero currently).

LARISSA BROWN is the author of sweeping love stories that cross time. Her novel, *Beautiful Wreck*, takes the reader from a bleak future to 10th-century Viking Iceland, a land of rugged beauty and ax-hewn justice. In addition to a companion novel, So Wild A Dream, Larissa has published one horror novella entitled Tress, and two knitting books with STC Craft. She's hard at work on a new love story that spans ten time periods and is learning about Medieval greyhounds and 18th-century automatons. See more at LarissaBrown.net

JACLYN WILMOTH grew up in the sultry swamps of Florida and developed a deep appreciation for the environment and how it shapes our experiences. Since then, she has taught English and art in Thailand, New Zealand, the Czech Republic, and the Bahamas. Her work appears in *Mid-American Review, The Dr. T.J. Eckleberg Review, Yemassee, Saw Palm*, and more. She earned an M.F.A. in Writing at the University of Alaska Fairbanks, where she now teaches creative writing. She is the co-editor of *Marrow Magazine* and the founder of *Lightning Droplets*.

EMILY FINHILL is a writer and full-time mom of four. At eleven, she started writing fairy stories to entertain her sisters, and things only got worse from there. A degree in English enabled her book addiction, and she's been blogging and writing short stories for ten years. Her first novel, *Meltdown*, is debuting one chapter at a time on *Medium*.

ELLE CAMPBELL lives in Wisconsin with her husband and three boys. Life as a #boymom often feels like living in a frat house for children, but she attempts to balance the copious amounts of testosterone by binge reading women's fiction and rom-coms. Currently, she's working on her first novel, a witchy story about rediscovering magic after trauma.

RARA RATBAG is a witch from the 7th circle of hell. She has been published over the past 6,020,075 years, and is still learning.

R.MINTER is an avid fiction reader and writer who lives in Texas. Her works have been published in *The Route 7 Review*, as well as a short story in *Share Your Scare Volume 5: A Lulu Anthology*. Her hope is to never stop learning and to polish her works into something ever better than the last.

MELISSA SASINA is a fantasy author from Ohio who is usually lost in her own imaginary worlds. Inspired by the words of her high school English teacher, Melissa decided to pursue her passion for the magical as an adult and has since published three series, *The Priestess Trilogy*, *The Chronicles of Midgard*, and *Darker Shade of Light*, as well as started a collection of short stories called *Tales from Earnia*. When not writing, she enjoys video and tabletop gaming, drawing, and procrastinating on the internet.

KIANA LIN is a writer, poet, and creative. A bit socially awkward, her words have always sounded better coming from her hands. To date, Kiana has self-published four books—and there are more on the way!

LISA WALTON is a storyteller, content strategist, and copywriter who believes the right words change lives. Lisa is innately curious and questions everything—a great trait for a writer but not for a movie date. She lives in Pennsylvania with her husband, three kids, and Sheepadoodles, Milo & Lucy. Learn more at lisamwalton.com.

So Many Thank Yous

To the writers who sent things even when it was scary.

To the moms who pushed to make a deadline they didn't think they could meet.

To the anthology team at Moms Who Write, who met an impossible turnaround for this book, while giving birth, having surgery, momming, working, and everything else. In no order at all: Brigid Levi, Abby Harding, Sarah Logan, Allison Wells, Shell Sherwood, Jill Robinson, Amber Turner, and Emily Scislowicz: You are the lifeblood of these projects, and we are all so grateful for the time and brain space you give every single week. We are so lucky to have you.

Brigid Levi. You pushed us when we were dragging. You hauled us over the finish line. This book would not exist without your dedication, your edits, and your insane commitment to this project. I have no idea how you did what you just did, but thank you. Thank you. Thank you.

Thank you to our families and friends who picked up slack when we were up late reading, editing, formatting, making graphics, and all of the other things that go into making books happen. We could not do it without all of you.

To the Moms Who Write group. You are supportive, creative, encouraging, and a million other adjectives that I can't even find right now. Thank you for showing up for each other. Thank you for submitting and reading and buying books. Thank you for existing.

~ Allie Gravitt

About Moms Who Write

Moms are creators. We create life. We create love. We create homes. And some of us create things with our words.
The catalyst for this project was my cry for friends who would get it. For other women who were trying to create and get the words and stories out of their heads. Who were struggling to fit everything in. Who were doing it all and still struggling to do anything.

So I reached out. And those people came.

It turns out there are so many of us. So many of us that scribble things on random pieces of paper or tap them into our phone notes or stay up way later than we should to get these words out of our heads. So many of us are fumbling through our creative process, trying to grow social media presences or hire an editor or figure out how the heck you even begin the query process. And when we come together, we are encouraged. We grow. We create.

It's really easy to believe that your words don't matter. That you're too busy and there just isn't time. That it's just too hard right now. And maybe it is. Or maybe we just need to know that we aren't alone and that there are hands on our backs.

I'm so proud to know these women. And we are so excited to invite you to join us as we tell our stories to the world.

You can find us at momswhowrite.org. Join our Facebook group. Follow us on social media and sign up for our mailing list to be a part of any upcoming anthology opportunities.

~ Allie Gravitt

The "Of Us" Series

Natural order is imperative for existence. Without it our world falls apart — we need leadership and food chains and circadian rhythms the way we need air. But what happens when we adopt an order that ISN'T natural? At some point, there will be a breakdown, and we will realize that there is a lot more to life than what we know. The boxes we put ourselves in suddenly feel too small, and the Order of Things feels a lot more negotiable. We fall apart, and eventually, we put ourselves back together. This is when we reclaim our beauty and our chaos. When we restore The Order of Us.

How much of us is born into our DNA and how much of it is a result of the people who raised us? Our values and priorities and prejudices and passions are all influenced by people around us. The people who hurt us or built us up. The people who introduced us to new ideas or challenged long-held beliefs.

They all matter, and they all change us.

Most of the time, though, stories are how we connect with other people. By sharing stories, you give other people the gift of your insight. You are giving people important reminders and hope.

Available wherever books are sold. All proceeds are donated.

Made in the USA
Middletown, DE
06 March 2023

26300456R00104